A Concealed Affection

Butterton Brides
Book 5

Ann Elizabeth Fryer

Copyright © June 5, 2025 by Ann Elizabeth Fryer

All rights reserved.

No portion of this book may be reproduced in any form without written permission from the publisher or author, except as permitted by U.S. copyright law.

AI was not used in the creation of this story.

For Annie Sotski, my enduring friend.

Trust in the Lord with all your heart, and lean not on your own understanding; in all your ways acknowledge Him and He shall direct your paths.

Proverbs 3:5-6

Chapter One

June, 1810

Tobias Chinworth entered the parlor, where I sat primly upon the settee. I was once a lady. I knew how to act the part. Yet, I stood at his entry as the servant I'd been portraying for the past few years...first with Emmaline in London. Now, here. At Mayfield Manor.

The wrinkle between Tobias's brows belied deep thought, his height entirely unaffected by the discouraged stoop in his shoulders. He bowed to me in acknowledgment. Neither of us stood on ceremony very often, not after what we'd been through. I waited for him to speak.

I knew what he meant to ask—what he'd already hinted upon. He turned to stand before the large window, his gaze unseeing. Was he remembering what I, too, could not forget? Compassion welled within me to near bursting. Was more than anyone's heart could take.

Never mind that he'd been despicable over the spring tide when he vied for dear Emmaline Carter's hand. His blasé comments to me were oft accompanied by a wink behind Emma's back and a twinkle in his eyes.

The man had been a flirt through and through. But now? Grief had drowned the flighty parts of him entirely, and I was seeing a truer Tobias Chinworth. One that had to reckon with the raw reality, and no flirtation, no diversion, no elaborate party could dull the pain. Such grief I, too, have known in my now distant past, though I be but five and twenty.

It has only been a few weeks since Mr. Chinworth, Tobias's father, returned with news of Samuel's death—and Mr. Chinworth's subsequent imprisonment. I was only vaguely aware of the charges as Joseph had left much out of the letter he'd sent to me. But to lose two brothers to an early grave, and a father to due demise, I couldn't fathom. Twas a shock that coursed through Butterton and all of London by now. The Banbury scandal had brought more than one gentleman to his knees; its scandalous tendrils reached far and wide.

Tobias stilled—the lavish mass of Grecian curls usually expertly tamed bespoke he'd been riding without his hat and at great speed. He took a deep breath and closed his eyes while I waited.

I'd been watching for Tobias the day that irrevocably changed his life. He'd agreed to help us—to help Joseph and Emma leave Mayfield Manor and Mr. Chinworth's machinations during the busy crush at the Butterton Hall ball.

He'd lost faith in his brother, Samuel. Despised his evil plans. Despised his father's manipulations. He'd sought his cousin Joseph for counsel.

We didn't count on little sister Cecily—the girl had a mind of her own and little knew the consequences her actions would take. She'd wanted to attend the ball, too, and had deceived her nurse concerning her medicine. She should have been sleeping.

If Cecily hadn't—if I had—oh, what could be done now? One couldn't simply turn back time and make different choices. I'd found her just before the first tragedy. I hid her face within my skirts, then gathered her in my arms and ran to the vicarage, away from the mayhem and Zacharay's crumpled body—accidentally killed by his drunken brother, Samuel. Later, I heard that Tobias tried to save his life. Tried and failed.

Tobias finally opened his eyes and turned to face me. I had to give him my answer. Today.

I had been waylaid by a new purpose over the last month. A sick, grieving girl clung to me and her last living brother lest we, too, leave her. I knew I could not. For all that was in my soul, I could not leave Cecily to her strange, new life alone. Motherless, Fatherless, but one surviving brother and few remaining household staff who didn't seem to care that she carried no spark of happiness and few companions to give her fellowship.

"Tessa." He waited, perspiration beading his upper lip. Twas a hot day, not fit for man or animal. Yet, he'd been out again, searching for his lost—mayhap stolen—infant nephew. "If it's about your salary..."

"It is not about that, as you well know." I hadn't meant for my voice to sound clipped or impatient.

"Yet, you hesitate." He tugged at his collar. "I would not blame you if you wanted to leave this cursed place."

No. That's not what I wanted. I wanted to gather him in my arms. Hold him. Comfort him. Heat burned my face at the thought. Compassion and love were two differing emotions. I'd best be careful.

Cecily had improved but little. My stay at Mayfield Manor seemed indeterminate, but my future was completely at my own will. I could live independently if I chose. My hesitation came from one single concern. My heart.

The more I've come to love the little imp, the more my heart has weakened towards her brother. If I stay, my heart might betray me and subsequently break me. I wasn't sure if I could handle another loss. My husband's death some years ago had been entirely unexpected. I'd grieved much. I tried ever so hard not to care for Tobias. Or love him. I was failing. Utterly.

He doesn't know. Must not know. And here I stand the fool for not giving the obvious answer. Vain thing I am to allow romance, or fear thereof, prevent me from doing what I knew to be right.

I curtsied. "I would be honored to continue with Cecily and am happy to attend her at your estate."

A flash of relief crossed his eyes. He needed me for Cecily. That was all. "Mayfield Manor has every comfort. But Burtins Hall is, shall we say, significantly more rustic." His voice lifted on a rare, positive note, "Will be cooler than here; I can vouch for that." He swiped sweat away with his handkerchief and unbuttoned his wool jacket. I wish protocol allowed him to dash it off in this infernal heat. I was thankful to be in short sleeves. "Give Cecily a change of scenery."

Gone was the cocksure gentleman that I'd observed when I first arrived with Emmaline last March. Here stood one changed by the gravity of life. How often had I seen him at war with himself as his brothers plotted and vied for my companion's hand?

When he wasn't flirting, he'd been downright cold. Other times, his soul leaked from his eyes when he didn't know I was watching.

Mayfield Manor had taken on quite a different mood since then. It was as though the entire estate knelt on its knees in repentance for its occupant's doings.

For one, Tobias had started attending church. The good vicar met with him often. And my step brother, Joseph Carter, now clasped his hand as a brother, rather than the indifferent cousin he'd been.

Who knew that a sudden partnership that one fateful night but one month past, would bring about my present occupation?

"Tessa? Of what do you think? There is a faraway look in your eyes. Are you sickened by this heat?" He threw open a window, and a blessed breeze filtered in.

"I never thought I'd—the past few months—" I hesitated to bring it all up again.

His eyelids lowered, and his mouth drew a line. "Tessa. I don't know what I would have done without you."

There it was. The wave of emotion in his voice would keep me pinned to my task of caring for his sister. At least until their lives could maintain a semblance of normalcy. Or until Tobias married. I would not stay then. Could not.

My heart must have bled into my expression.

"You do not believe me?" His gaze was sincere, to be sure. I did believe him. That I was useful—helpful. Regarded with respect. But anything else? I'd have to conceal my heart better than this. Besides, I had no business losing my heart to this rogue. No matter how repentant he may be.

"I am happy to be of service." Service. Would that be the only thing I'd be good for anymore? I had chosen this path, after all. I could be the weary widow doing nothing but existing within four walls if I desired.

A strange look came over his face. "I ought not keep the full truth from you, Tessa."

I swallowed at the lump in my throat. "I daresay not." What more could be said? The truth and more truth could turn lives quite another direction. Would that be the case?

He nodded. "I didn't want to tell you, but I think it best. I don't feel we are safe here. I feel—watched. Spied upon." He put his hand in his pocket. "I found this. On Father's desk in his study."

He handed the missive to me. "A threat has been made. The constable believes I should take it seriously given the circumstances of Father's crimes and Samuel's tragic rampage..."

I unfolded the paper. *"The Chinworth name will fall in the rubble of its stone. Not one will remain. Pay or die."* My hand slipped to my throat. "Horrible...and confusing!"

He shook his head. "To be entirely honest, though it goads my pride to say it, there isn't much in the way of finances. Personally, I've naught but what little my estate brings in."

"Is there an outstanding debt?" Such a strange request—payment or death. Pay whom?

Tobias grunted. "I cannot find evidence of debt, but that doesn't mean there isn't. And how should I know who to pay? Ambiguity doesn't help the matter, does it? I'd ask Father but he won't speak to me—won't answer any of my questions. He told me to leave Mayfield. Indeterminately."

"You trust that command?" Perchance the note was intended for his father instead. Tobias needed to shave. The dark shadow of a beard gave his boyish features a roguish cast. He wasn't getting much sleep either.

He shrugged. "In light of this?" He pulled the note from my hands. "I have nowhere else to go. Besides, it's high time I looked after my estate. I'm not doing my father's bidding any longer. I couldn't. Not after everything. But what I can do is get you and Cecily somewhere safe. I feel it—I don't know why, but I feel it is the right move to make."

So, we'd go to Burtin's Hall. Twenty miles north of here. Perhaps Cecily would do as we hoped. She'd heal. And Tobias... he had truly changed. So much. And yes, my heart was at risk—regardless of my determination to remain a mere servant to his sister. But, could I really trust the man? Many reformed gentlemen fell back into old habits. It could happen.

Ah, well. Time would tell. And if I was in any danger, I smirked; I could defend myself, even without weapons. Thanks to Joseph's training.

"You find our situation humorous?" Tobias's brows rose.

"No indeed, Mr. Chinworth. I merely smile in the face of the future."

"I wish I had your enthusiasm."

"We've already come through the worst, don't you think?"

He took a step closer and halted; his eyes grew warm. "When I find Samuel's child alive, I may learn to hope again." He shook his head. "I know not where else to search. I wouldn't stop; except I'd rather be alive to raise the lad when he is found. Lord Sherborne assures me my absence will not stall his assistance to find the babe, but..." his voice trailed off.

I put my hand on his arm. "Of course. I pray each day for his return." How could a babe disappear so easily? It was a conundrum none of us could figure out.

"Samuel didn't deserve him..." Tears smarted his eyes, but he did not try to hide or wipe them away. "Is he still alive? I do not know. How can I explain my affection for a babe I've never met?"

I had no words but stayed by his side. His left hand rose slowly and cupped my cheek. My heart thrummed at his nearness. Did he care? Like that?

"Don't stop praying, Tessa."

"I won't."

I felt a stab of guilt at the doubt I'd entertained. Tobias Chinworth was a changed gentleman. I could trust him.

"Tessa..." he whispered. His voice, low and husky.

I swallowed.

"I meant what I said, I—" A scream split us apart.

Cecily was awake.

Chapter Two

Dr. Rillian said it would take time for Cecily's body to readjust to not being dosed with that awful concoction that kept her asleep much of the day. As much as he hated to do so, we had to keep giving the strange medicine to her, but in lesser doses, a decrease each week.

When the bottles were empty, we would toss the lot of them into the lake and celebrate. Cecily might one day enjoy a normal childhood like she ought to have. As it were, her latest tirade—agitations set off by a lower dose of medicine this week—left us exhausted. Settling her took both of us.

Betimes she anxiously desired to find Samuel, her favorite brother. A brother who'd manipulated her as much as she tried to manipulate everyone else. A poor hero he'd made. Tobias faulted himself for not giving her enough attention. He faulted himself for much these days.

We sat upon her bed, the child finally, blissfully, asleep between us. Tobias leaned against the headboard with his eyes shut, but I knew he was awake. How many times had we done this?

Entirely improper. But we had no choice. Most of the house help had abandoned Mayfield when the scandal began. And Cecily wouldn't allow anyone else near her. Dr. Rillian took it in stride. Propriety was far less important than a little girl's life. I agreed. How often had we sat in the parlor or library with naught but each other? With no chaperone for decency? There was also the fact that we called each other by our Christian names. I do not even know how or when it began.

To say we knew a certain modicum of intimacy was an understatement. His future wife would be none too pleased if she found it out. My jaw clenched. I mustn't think of that. He wasn't thinking of taking a wife. Was not engaged. And I, I...

"Tessa..." Tobias whispered in the darkening room. "Go take your rest."

"If you are sure?"

He cocked a brow and pointed to the water pitcher.

I eased myself from Cecily's side, her long golden hair slipped from my arm to her pillow. She took a deep breath but did not wake. I quietly poured a tumbler of water and handed it to him.

"Thank you."

"Need you anything stronger?"

"Do not tempt me. I've given it up."

Did he, now? "Tea then?"

He reached for my hand and squeezed. "You are an angel."

"I'll be back."

I left the door slightly ajar and made my way to the kitchen. The cook had been instructed to allow me liberties within her space, as I had to daily ensure Emma received tea that wasn't tainted with laudanum or—the dangerous elixir Mr. Chinworth thought was helping his daughter. I did the same for Tobias. Trust among the family and staff was thin.

Making a fresh pot was calming work. A blessing. Thankfully, the cook knew the routine and always left a kettle of water to heat. I poured hot water into the brown teapot and let the tea leaves steep.

These quiet moments after Cecily calmed enough to sleep were almost sacred. A relief, to be sure. A surety that storms always died down, and something better would come next. I poured cream and tea into the cup and made my way back to Tobias. I'd return for a solitary cup of my own.

He met me in the hall, quietly closing Cecily's door. "I think she's out cold. It has to be exhausting, causing so much ruckus."

I handed him his tea with a slight rattle on the saucer, his finger accidentally grazed my thumb, leaving a trail of heat. His eyes captured mine as they had earlier in the parlor. As though he felt more—and would say more, but did not.

He offered a light bow. "Rest well, Tessa."

"I thank you, I shall."

He lifted his cup in a resigned salute and made his way to his room.

What would he have said had he allowed his lips to follow his thoughts? Did I want to know? I needed to be careful lest I read in his expressions something untrue. *Careful, Tessa. You must be careful...*

I slipped back down the long flight of steps to the kitchen and made my own cup of tea. Creamy, soothing. Was there anything better? I poured a second after I drank the first and made my way back to my room. I stalled to listen at Cecily's door. All quiet. Thank God.

Until tomorrow then, dear girl. We shall keep pushing ahead and one day you will move past this strange season of your life... it will be a distant scene and nothing more...

A shuffling sounded, then a loud grunt. Surely, she hadn't woken? But that was not a sound the child would make. Another strained and unrefined grunt filtered down the hall—from Tobias's room. Was he ill?

I ran as fast as I could to his door. The sounds grew louder as I approached. I hesitated, my hand gripping the knob. What if I caught him with his shirt off? And nothing wrong with him but spilled tea? A voice hissed and something heavy dropped to the ground. I had to know if Tobias was alright. Nothing for it...

I shoved through the door, swallowing a scream. Twas so dark—no candle had been lit. But I could see a hulking form wrestling in the center of the room. Two men were fighting! I had to think quickly and clearly.

I couldn't tell who was who until Tobias was shoved to the bed, his shirt most definitely off. His eyes flicked to mine, but the other man didn't see me. The stranger lifted a pistol and took a few steps back. He'd caught his prey, so he thought.

The stranger was about my height. What had Jospeh said about disarming from behind? Oh yes. I could handle this villain. Indeed.

The stranger spoke through gritted teeth. "I'm going to kill you!"

"What?" Tobias flicked his chin. "No chance to pay?" He shot a glance at me that I ignored. Warning me off?

That was it, I'd wait no longer. In a swift action, I drew close, buckling the man's knees with my own. I wrenched his arm behind his back, swiping the pistol with more ease than when I'd practiced with Joseph. He'd not seen me enter the room. Clearly.

The man swore as he turned to face a new enemy. "A woman! What's a woman—give it here," he swiped the air to grab the pistol, "if you know what's good for you." His accent belied the streets of London.

I cocked the hammer—a double barrel—and aimed at his rugged form—a patchy head of hair, bristly beard. And such stench!

His eyes glinted. "Give it here."

He reached for me, but I backed up. The pistol was heavy, but I would hold fast.

Tobias skirted around the edge of the bed and waved. "Toss it to me."

I ignored him. I mustn't give this villain even a sliver of a chance. I aimed. "I'm an expert shot, mind you. Best you sit in that chair if you wish your heart to beat come midnight."

The man lunged for me again and I shot, two inches left, into his arm. As planned. His eyes widened in shock as he stumbled backward, cursing as blood spilled down his arm.

Tobias's well-muscled chest heaved from the exertion. "You best do as she tells you."

The man glanced at the gun he'd supplied himself with, blinked twice at his wound, and fainted instead, clattering to the floor as a knife jangled from his other hand. I hadn't seen it. And that could have cost us.

"Tessa." Tobias folded his arms. "I see my cousin has trained more than men at his estate."

"Quite."

"But you are a woman. Why would you need..." His eyes darkened as he stood—a head taller over me. "I should have been the one to protect you."

"I wasn't the one being accosted." My heart was going to beat out of my chest. My hands began to shake.

"True." He lit a candle and held it to the man's face. Blood began to pool beneath him, soaking into the rug. "I will send for the constable."

"Tobias?"

"Yes?" He lifted the candle and stood.

"I need help."

Confusion flit across his face.

"I can't seem to unlock my hand from the gun." My voice began to shake too. While I was indeed an expert shot, I'd never shot into flesh before now. The experience had me in dizzy waves of something I'd never dealt with.

He came beside me and clasped both hands around mine, turning the barrel away. "You did well. You can let go now. Breathe, Tessa."

I took a deep breath. What had Joseph said to do? My thoughts muddled. Sweat trickled down my temples. Tobias's hands eased the pistol from mine as weakness overtook me. This would never do.

"I've never seen someone—I've never seen a *woman* act so bravely." He placed the pistol beside him on the table. "The way you threw him off balance before disarming him...my question is, why? Why does Tessa know how to do these things? Why did my cousin train you?"

He stepped away and grabbed his shirt, pulling it on, along with his vest.

I glanced at the villain. There was more blood. Mayhap I killed the man after all. One could bleed to death after all. I grabbed the bedpost for balance as a wave of dizziness beset me. I was not prepared for Tobias's next question.

"Who are you really, Tessa?"

I shut my eyes and took a clean breath. He may as well know. It was only fair if he depended on me to care for Cecily. "I am the widow of a man who was murdered. I have been spied upon, chased. I've had to stand at my husband's grave whom I loved with my life, though young I was. And I will never be in a vulnerable position in the face of evil ever again. Ever."

"Your connection with my cousin?"

"Stepsister, of a sort."

"Of a sort?"

"Our parents married...before their deaths. Years ago."

"Ah. I knew Uncle had remarried. I'd never met his new wife." He refolded his arms. "You are a widow."

"I am."

"How long were you married?"

My jaw clenched at his questions. "But two years…"

"Such a short time."

It was. Too short.

"I shouldn't be calling you Tessa. It's Mrs…"

"Smith."

"You are lying."

"Yes. I cannot go by my married name. I must not."

"Hiding?"

I knew too much. And *they* knew that.

"The man is moving…" Tobias swiped his abandoned cravat from the floor and went to work. "Are you able to alert Jenkins to ride for the constable?"

"Indeed." I could do so. I must. I willed my legs to walk to the door.

"And Mrs. Smith?"

I flinched.

"Please…"

He did not look at me.

"Will you check on Cecily? The gunfire may have woken her."

"At once, Mr. Chinworth."

And thus, the closeness between us seemed quite ended.

I sent Jenkins to the constable, checked on the sleeping child, crawled atop my bed and wept. An hour later, a hand snaked into mine. A pair of eyes gazed upon me. A handkerchief pressed against my face in soft touches.

Tobias.

"I've brought you some tea. See? Doctor Rillian has come to look after you."

Dr. Rillian drew to my side. "Are you well, child?"

I rose and sat on the edge of the bed. "Merely heart sore."

He nodded. "Tis a difficult action to put lead into a man, be it necessary." His kind eyes soothed.

"Will he live?" I needed to know, but wasn't sure if I should ask. Did I really want to know?

"Aye. For now. He's been hauled off to the gaol. Cat's got his tongue. Won't say who paid him for the attack."

I shut my eyes at the implications.

"Drink your tea, Tessa." Tobias used my name again. My heart warmed. He nestled the cup into my hands.

I lifted it to my lips and tried to swallow it but the liquid wouldn't go down. I rushed to the wash basin and lost my supper. Dr. Rillian followed and gave support to my heaving shoulders. "That's right. Let it out, my girl. Let it out. You'll feel better soon."

Some minutes later, I lay atop the bed, weak and embarrassed. Tobias had seen everything. I wasn't the heroine he thought me.

"Send for her maid, man. Don't just stand there. I require some hot water as well."

I had no maid. As for the hot water...Tobias gave a curt nod and left.

"I think a sleeping draught is in order." He smiled. "I've helped many a youth through his first shot. Too many battles, too many wars..."

"Must I? What if Cecily needs me?"

He nodded. "The medicine will calm your stomach—and I promise to stay and help look after the child. You need to rest."

"Alright." I couldn't disagree. I was weak from tip to toe.

Tobias returned with the kitchen's steaming kettle, a towel around his arm, looking more like a servant than a master. To think a Chinworth performing such menial tasks.

I washed my face in the fresh hot water, then the draught was mixed and given to me. A blanket was spread across my form as I grew drowsy. I blinked in the darkness, my hands locking and unlocking against the imaginary pistol I held in my thoughts.

Tobias leaned over me. Was he angry? I couldn't bear it. He leaned closer and pressed his lips against my forehead. My heart cinched at his touch...

"Sleep, Tessa," he said as he softly shut the bedroom door behind him.

Then I was alone. Alone in my dreams, quiet, soft, silent. Healing.

I woke to their voices, how many hours later? I blinked to sunlight—bright, hot sunlight. Must be well past noon. They stood in my doorway talking.

"I've never seen a woman leverage her body in such a way as to disarm a man, she—she saved my life."

Amusement laced Dr. Rillian's tone. "And this bothers you?"

"How can a female have beauty, common sense, and strength?"

Dr. Rillian laughed. "You haven't known enough women."

"I don't doubt there are strong women, but Tessa is a lady. She is gentle."

My heart sped and I shut my eyes lest they knew I overheard.

"A gentlewoman with abilities. Fancy that." Doctor Rillian moved closer. "She told you of her past?"

"She did. Some."

"You can't blame her."

"Blame her? No indeed. I do not. I am glad of it. Merely, I am astounded by last night's rescue."

I could still hear the wonder in Tobias's voice. He was glad? But he'd called me Mrs. As though...

"Good."

Silence accompanied their footsteps to my bedside. My eyes fluttered open and I focused on their faces. My limbs felt heavy, but my mind was becoming quite clear.

"Now, young lady." Dr. Rillian pulled a pouch off his arm. "When you are ready for the day, I believe," he lifted the flap and removed a pistol, "that the best medicine for you will be some target practice."

I rose to a sitting position, protesting. "I couldn't!"

Dr. Rillian smiled. "You must get back on the horse, as Joseph would say."

I took a breath and caught the smile lighting Tobias's face. "I quite agree," he said, "and I will be joining you."

"What about Cecily?" The last thing she needed was several rounds of gunfire in her ears.

"Elaina and Callum have taken her on a picnic to Goodwyn Abbey. She'll be gone most of the day. That will give us time to pack for Burtins. We leave in the morning, Tessa."

Chapter Three

We packed with all haste, the work taking the remainder of the day. How much did a girl of eleven years of age need? We made our best guess. As we worked, the threat loomed. Someone was out to see the Chinworth name ground into the dust.

It very nearly had been. We bundled Cecily into the carriage while it was still dark and embarked on our journey to Burtins Hall. If the roads were good and the horses didn't go lame, we'd arrive by nightfall.

Angelic Cecily had fallen asleep against my shoulder; her feet curled beneath a blanket though it was a warm day. She took the news of our departure with unexpected enthusiasm. I daresay her adventurous spirit was ready to see what lay outside the walls of Mayfield.

"You managed to hit the targets well, Tessa." Tobias nodded with approval.

I'd been shaky at first, but regained composure with the very real thought that my training had come into good use, and may yet again.

"Almost as good as me." He snickered. "I take it you own a pistol?" He pointed his chin to the pouch I'd slipped behind a cushion.

"Not a double barrel. Indeed." One more befitting a woman's hand.

He stroked his chin and shook his head. "I've got a bluestocking for a governess."

The two words stung. Bluestocking and governess. I was neither. "Is it progressive for a woman to be able to defend herself?"

"I think—" He quirked his lips. "I think that men ought to be at all times protectors of women. A woman should never have to be her own savior."

"High thinking indeed."

He leaned forward. "It doesn't follow that all men have that honor, does it? I didn't. At one time. Not that I've ever harmed a lady. Not in that way." He shifted in his seat, uncomfortable. "What I'm trying to say is that men should do better. Be better." He smiled. "Having said that, I am glad you saved me. You'll have to show me that trick with the knees."

Not a hard one. "Spend a few weeks at Joseph's estate. Will be worth the effort."

"I may do just that." He tapped his fingers on his knee. "But do tell." His voice softened. "I pray you weren't present at your husband's demise?"

Of course he'd be curious. I didn't blame him for it. Not when I'd been rather mysterious about the whole affair. I answered him. "No."

Tobias's brow rose at my lack of information. Joseph had been the one to find my husband in the shipyard. He'd been at the wrong place at the wrong time. Patrick had gone to collect a payment for his employer. Joseph found my husband's lifeless body propped beneath the deck.

I shut my eyes against the memory I'd imagined time and again.

The memory of Joseph banging down my door, of the men that had followed him. Of the fight that ensued. How I'd been useless when Joseph needed help and was knocked cold. My hands had been tied as the men searched my home, taking anything and everything valuable along with papers from Patrick's office. They left with a threat.

Tobias touched my hand and I startled. "What harm has come to you?" Real concern lit his expression.

I'd almost been taken advantage of. Almost. Joseph woke. And so did his fury.

I swallowed. "Joseph handled it. Before...before..." I couldn't say the words.

"That is why he trained you. I surmised as much." He loosened his cravat. "I am sorry that happened to you. More than I can say."

I don't know why, but I wanted to cry just then. The man I was trying not to love, caring this much. I'd never told anyone the whole truth of what had happened that day. Only Joseph knew. Was safer that way.

"How long ago did your tragedy occur?"

I'd been but nineteen. "Nearly six years ago."

"Has your heart healed?"

My heart? To love again? Would that it had not. "I will always regard my departed husband with a loving memory. I cannot help but do so. I have reconciled myself with his death, yes." But my heart? My heart had become vulnerable within days of Tobias's own tragedy and change. The walls I'd put up had fallen with great ease.

I could indeed protect myself. My heart? This remained to be seen.

Tobias had more questions. "The name you've taken...Smith, I believe you said this is to protect you from the people that killed your husband?"

"And perhaps his employer. We are certain he was involved, but there was little evidence. A very little." There were things we knew but couldn't tangibly confirm or provide to the law.

"One cannot be too careful."

I shrugged. "Joseph put me to work looking after Emmaline. I was still in London, but very much secluded. We did not socialize at all. Before, when I was married, I moved about the lower social circles. I wasn't widely known, truth be told." At least that's what I told myself.

I'd married for love, to a man that chose to work. He despised the idle life of a gentleman. I'd been included in card parties out of regard for my beloved deceased parents.

"But your surname? I suppose it recognizable or you would not need to borrow such a common one."

I bit the side of my cheek. Smith was the easiest option. Patrick's death had made the papers. I had no reason not to tell him. Twas old news. Those events had happened long enough ago. "My name was Contessa Auldlington."

Tobias startled. "You were married to Patrick Auldlington?"

A small alarm ran within. "Did you know him?"

He shook his head in a slow motion. "No. I did not."

I don't know why that relieved me so. But why had he startled? Cecily awakened, ending that particular conversation. The remainder of the journey consisted of her incessant chattering and questions about Burtins. I'd not seen her so animated, so enthused since I'd come to know her.

Tobias offered me a smile. Smiles bespoke hope. He might not recognize it yet but hope was returning to his soul—or rather—finding a home there for the first time. I smiled back.

I knew from experience that difficulties were temporary. We'd much to live for, much joy to accumulate in our futures, despite the shocking events that played out last month.

If I could do anything, it would be to give Tobias and Cecily joy.

We arrived just as the sun splayed its final rays upon the earth, indeed, the splendor that belonged to Derbyshire quite took my breath. This was truly a change of scenery. We pulled through ancient stone gates to Burtins Hall, built of the same. Thick and grey, tall and narrow. A quarter of Mayfield Manor's size.

But one window gleamed with candlelight.

"The housekeeper will be none too pleased that I did not warn her of our arrival." He smiled. "But not for long."

A young boy ran toward the horses—his eyes were wide with surprise at our arrival, and then an aged caretaker stumbled through the front door and toward the carriage. The man was drunk, and as we disembarked, another shadow of a horse and rider fled into the distance.

"Entertaining this eve, are we, Cummins? Tobias stood more than a head taller than the weaving, stooped man.

"Eh? Master Chinworth? Naught but cards. Join me, man? See if you'll besht me this night? Ye can tosh yer mistress fer later, ye ken."

My face flamed.

Tobias shoved him. "This lady is no mistress, you wretch. She is a lady and must be treated as such."

The man swiped his hat from his balding head. "Pardon...pardon, ma'am. He ain't never took a mistress, don't rightly know why, mind ye. Thought he come to 'is manhood finally." A laugh followed a belch.

"Sleep it off, we shall have words in the morning." Tobias shoved him away from us. "To the stables with you, man!"

Cummins tipped his hat again and wove his way toward the stables.

Tobias was angry. "Tessa—that was inexcusable. I will dismiss him in the morning. Please forgive me."

Cecily jumped from the carriage step. "Tobias? Is it safe here?"

"Come—" he gathered his sister in his arms. "We are safe. Cummins didn't know we were coming and had too much to drink. But I will set him straight. No fear." We shared a look. While he'd reassured his sister, both of us were yet wary.

A berobed woman of some years flew from the doorway bearing a lantern. "Master Chinworth!" She smiled wide, come in, lad! And who do ye have with ye? Can this be the wee babe grown?" Cecily shrank behind us.

"Lucky for you I have drinking chocolate." She winked at Cecily. "Do come have some, will you? The cocoa was a gift from the good vicar."

"Brilliant, Mrs. Fredrickson. Sounds just the thing."

"I'll have the lads bring in your trunks. I take it Cummins was in the cups again?" She shook her head. "Man won't heed my warning. And between you and me, I don't like the company he keeps of late."

"Mrs. Smith," He gestured to me, "Burtins' housekeeper extraordinaire. Place would be in shambles without her."

The woman offered me a kind smile. "You the governess for the child?"

Tobias took my hand and placed it in the crook of his arm. "Both a generous companion and a lady, mind you. She will be treated as such."

Fredrickson curtsied. "At your service, Miss. I will heat the chocolate then set about readying your rooms."

Indeed, the woman emanated goodness itself. I could not help but instantly like her.

Tobias led me through a low arched door that led into a dark foyer, and through another arched door. A dingy hall, miniscule compared to Mayfield Manor's, with furnishings that seemed of an ancient make. He had warned me Burtin's to be a rustic place.

Cecily dashed about, peering into the swiftly darkening rooms. Plaster had thinned to the point that stone peeked through. A coat of arms, one I did not recognize, hung above the fireplace. Three dogs were represented, looking much like the Irish wolfhounds we'd left at Mayfield. "Loyalty, faithfulness, protection..." the words *lux vitae* carved below the fierce heads. *Light of life...* much nuance in the two simple words placed together, and seemingly in the darkest corner.

"Good idea, Tessa." He folded his arms and gazed at the beasts. "I will acquire some dogs on the morrow. To help look out for us." He glanced about as though a guest and not its owner. "This estate belonged to my mother's brother, who died without children. Twas provided for me." He shrugged. "I am ashamed I've done little here."

His shame would never end.

I placed my hand on his arm. "But you are here now. Ready to do some good, I think."

"If a Chinworth can be of any good...I will do my best."

I sat on a faded chair by a cold hearth. The housekeeper brought in the chocolate, quickly served us, and lit a few candles about the room. "Give me an hour, Master Chinworth, and you three can retire for the night."

I followed Tobias' gaze to the flickering candle flame. A chill draft blew in and snuffed it out. Cecily cried, "Ghost!" She clutched onto me and trembled. Much as she had done that night—the night Zachary had died.

I snapped my gaze to the doorway. A man lingered, a deathly pallor to his sunken cheeks. His graying dressing gown and nightcap contrasted with a long white beard that flowed down his chest.

"What's this?" His chin trembled. "My own flesh and blood come to grace Burtins Hall? To what gain for yourself?" His accusation must be meant for Tobias. But why?

Tobias stood, confused. "What on earth? Uncle! I was under the impression that you had—that you—" He was utterly bewildered. "What is going on here?"

The man seemed amused. "What? That I'd died? Your father wishes it, to be sure."

"But the death notice came and your name was on it. Yours. None other."

The man grunted. "Death notice? He cocked his chin. "Come to do me in have you? Playing the Grim Reaper for your dear old father?"

"Of course not. Why would Father wish you gone? Indeed, you attach to him a violence he is not capable of."

Yet, I could see the question in Tobias's eyes. Was his father capable of murder? He was imprisoned and awaiting trial for a past wrong but not that particular form of evil. If a man was capable of one kind of vile deed, then mayhap another.

The old uncle spat. "And yet he molders in the gaol, does he not?"

Tobias tossed me a quick glance. "I saw your death notice. Was even in the London papers. I swear to you, I read it with my own eyes."

He folded his berobed arms. "How long ago was this?"

"But two months past."

"Why didn't you care to come see me buried yourself, eh?" He pointed to Tobias, but looked at me. "You see how he cares not for his own relation. Bah." He clicked his teeth, or what remained of them, as the kind housekeeper gently pushed him aside from blocking the doorway.

"Mr. Mulls, you are out of bed and like to catch your death."

"You want me to die too, is that it?"

"Posh man. Get you back to bed. You aren't well enough yet, and the injury has yet to heal."

Tobias started. "Injury? What kind of injury?"

Mr. Mulls's nightcap slipped, revealing long gray strands of hair. "My dear boy, at exactly two months past, Burtins was robbed and I was shot."

A robbery too. How shocking!

Tobias seemed at loose ends. And too tired to deal with more problems. "What was stolen that was worth such an injury? There's hardly anything valuable here."

The housekeeper grimaced as she counted on fingers. "One, the saltbox, two, the sugar box, and," she hesitated, "three the *silver box*."

"You've got to be kidding me. I understand the value of silver, but who would risk all for salt and sugar?"

To one who lived a privileged life, salt and sugar must seem like nothing.

Mulls pressed a hand to his chest. "I was shot defending your precious silver, boy. About paid with my life so you might eat like a rich lad whilst here. Don't know why or how a death notice came of the incident."

Cecily's grip tightened as she pressed her face to my side. "Mr. Chinworth, I believe your sister might need a *good* story and a long rest after today's long journey." I grew increasingly concerned about Cecily's probable unrest—potentially a long, disturbed night ahead if they kept this discussion up. Such topics wouldn't be good if she were here to heal. "What say you?"

He nodded but continued despite my subtle warning to stop the fearsome talk. "Why would someone wish to make the world believe you'd died?"

"Bah, I do not know. I'm of no value to dear Albion or beyond."

The housekeeper placed a hand on each hip. "Nonsense, Mr. Mulls. The village children think you are an absolute angel. Now off to bed with you."

"Mrs. Fredrickson, I do not look an angel." He turned back to Tobias. "We shall have words, Tobias Chinworth. Come morning." He turned and left the room.

Cecily tugged Tobias's jacket. "Samuel came here. Two months ago. He told me to keep it a secret."

Tobias turned at her words, concern lining his face. "Did he? How did you find out about it?"

She cocked her head to the side as though he were daft. "Same way I find out anything. I sneaked and listened in."

I could tell he was trying to keep his surprise hidden. Not that either of us could be entirely shocked by her shenanigans of the past months. "Did you? And did he give you a present for keeping quiet?"

Her face colored pink. "I didn't know anyone would get hurt. Is it my fault?"

"No, child. Not at all. Don't even think that way." Tobias and I shared another look.

She'd been taught to lie and manipulate. Rewarded for it. And had experienced firsthand the darkness of such dealings. Since then, she'd been working so hard at being honest an honest girl—no more lying. I believed she told the truth. There would be no recompense for her except for our trust, which she desired above all.

But what had Samuel been doing here? It wasn't his estate to be concerned about. And was it he that shot at this aged distant uncle? And stole the salt, sugar, and silver? So strange. My mind ran away with me. Samuel was guilty of bad things. That didn't also mean he was guilty of shooting at his uncle.

We were whisked away to our rooms with the greater question following the heels of every thought. Were we truly safe here?

Chapter Four

I awoke to the sound of a full tray crashing down the stairs, or so I guessed.

Mrs. Fredrickson's voice could be heard, "You silly goose, you've overfilled it and lost your balance. Mr. Mulls has no use for three jam pots, he only eats strawberry," she tsked. "Try again, dear. And consider how uneven the steps are. You must memorize them if you are to be of any use in this house."

A younger voice responded. "Yes, Missus. I am sorry. I will try again."

Twas a maid in training. I glanced at Cecily still sleeping in the smaller bed positioned across from mine. The sound had not disturbed her. The room, of the same patchy stone and plaster, was nonetheless cozy.

Mrs. Fredrickson had gone through the trouble of putting us in one of the better rooms, she'd said. The linens however, must have resided in the depths of a trunk amid aged bundles of lavender for a very long time and the curtains, I fingered the dark green wool, were moth-eaten. I didn't imagine Burtins Hall entertained guests, if ever.

I washed my face in an old cracked bowl and put up my hair before a much-spotted mirror. I dressed myself and left Cecily snuggled beneath her blankets. She was exhausted from the previous day and received a small dose of the dreaded elixir later in the evening than usual. She likely wouldn't wake until noon.

Thank goodness Mr. Mulls's recounting hadn't frightened her too much. I'd bundled her in her softest gown, told her a story, and helped her with her prayers. A new experience, as she didn't know anyone except the vicar was free to pray to God.

I closed the door softly and made my way down the narrow, winding steps. Breakfast in the dining room—down to the left, Tobias had said.

A narrow sideboard held a few covered dishes, the table entirely empty. Had Tobias already eaten? I had a dozen questions to ask him. But mayhap it was none of my business. I was here to help rehabilitate Cecily and be her companion. Not to sort out his family dramas, which seemed to keep us all guessing.

"Oh good. I hoped you would be awake." Tobias. He offered me a smile. "Sleep well?" Dark shadows yet stained beneath his eyes.

"Well enough. I daresay better once I become accustomed to the bed."

"Rather lumpy, was it?" He grimaced.

"I've slept in worse."

"I'll send for new mattresses." He pulled a piece of foolscap from his pocket and penciled a note. "Dogs, food, mattresses—anything you might require?"

Twas like we were housekeeping. Together, for real. It sent a pang in my heart. I noted his untamed hair, his shadow of a beard.

"I might require a comb for your hair, Mr. Chinworth."

He grinned. "My valet has quite been lax, I'm afraid."

I smiled back at his attempt at humor. His valet had abandoned Mayfield when the troubles began. He hadn't bothered acquiring a new one.

"But point taken. I will see to this mane of mine before the village sees me in such a state." His voice lowered. "For some reason, I do not feel ashamed of it before you, Tessa."

I'd seen him flirt before. Shamelessly. This was pure honesty. Mayhap with a little flirtation. Mayhap...

He ran a hand through his hair, creating a high fluff. "I do believe I should know how to care for myself as well as you can. To be self reliant is of great value, I'm finding."

"It can be, yes." I tried not to laugh at his disheveled state—he still looked handsome. Unbearably so.

"Here, let me serve your breakfast." He began to take the lids from the bowls. "What has Mrs. Fredrickson scraped together for us?"

Delicious scent invaded the room. I admit I was ravenous.

"Well done. We've eggs, bacon, and porridge—a pot of jam, brambleberry, no doubt." He lifted a plate, scooped generous portions, and set it before me.

The housekeeper walked in. "Master Chinworth! Ye'll not be serving while at Burtins! You leave me the work to do." She set a steaming teapot upon the table. Hot creamy tea sounded like Heaven.

Tobias rejoined, "My good housekeeper, if she wishes to remain employed, will allow me this freedom, if unusual."

She blinked in confusion, but he gave her no chance to respond. "I'm beginning to think a master is no master unless he knows how to serve. I begin here. With Tessa." A soft smile played about his lips. If Emma had seen and come to know this kind of Tobias, would she have chosen him out of the three brothers? I wouldn't have blamed her. I shook the thought. Joseph was always meant to be hers. That was plain to see.

Mrs. Fredrickson harrumphed. "As you wish. However, I will pour the tea. You will not deprive me of that honor, sir." She winked at me.

Such an agreeable woman. I liked her very much.

"I thank you," I told them both. "For the breakfast and the tea." I unfolded my napkin and spread it across my lap. "How is Mr. Mulls this morning?"

"Ah yes, how is my cantankerous, living, breathing uncle?"

"Aye, he's peaceful now that you're here. You might attend him when you get the chance."

Tobias nodded. "I planned to do just that." He filled his plate and sat across from me. "Thank you, Fredrickson."

She curtsied and left the room.

"Is Mr. Mulls the rightful owner of Burtins?"

"No indeed. He isn't my mother's brother, but her deceased sister's husband. She made provision for him to live here."

I thought of the opulence of Mayfield Manor. Would he not be better cared for there? But thinking upon its recent inhabitants, perhaps not.

"Has he no living?"

"For a fifth son who married a third daughter—no. It is my understanding he hasn't a farthing left to him." He took a bite of bacon. "But he hasn't been entirely idle. The man has an affinity for kite making."

"Kite making?" I did not expect that. I hadn't flown a kite in years.

Tobias pointed. "His workshop is on the uppermost floor. Sells them to a shop in Manchester and often will gift the village children with them on a birthday."

Mr. Mulls might be a more thoughtful man than I'd first given him credit for. "I hope he makes one for Cecily."

"I daresay she would enjoy it." Tobias lifted a forkful of eggs and chewed. "I wonder if it was Samuel who shot him. But—I cannot reconcile why he would need salt, sugar, and my silver for that matter. Makes no sense. Not with his overflowing bank account. Why on earth would he come here in the first place?"

"No. It doesn't make sense." Nothing about Samuel had. Why would anyone choose such dark doings over good? Ah, but the devil plays a deceptive game of smoke and mirrors and ploys for self-importance. He'd fallen prey to it—as many have. Thank God Tobias hadn't.

"What of the strange death notice—and in the London papers?" Tobias lifted his hands in exasperation. "I'm only ashamed I didn't try to attend the supposed funeral. I would have known something was off a little sooner."

What had I thought just a second ago? "Smoke and mirrors." I set my fork down. "A distraction. The things that were stolen? A mere cover for another theft. Someone must have taken something—mayhap something important, but wanted the focus to be on what's obviously missing."

"Tessa. What you say may be true, but there has never been anything important here. Not within Burtins Hall, or on the property." He chewed his bacon slowly. "That I know of, which is very little. It's not like I've really invested myself in the place. Samuel kept me busy—and—Father—and…" His face clouded as new realizations dawned. "They kept me too busy to come here. Mocked it at times. Surely Father…" He let the thought trail unfinished.

But I knew what he meant to say. Mr. Chinworth's actions had been unfortunate. Had been tangled up with the likes of Banbury. A past mistake that rued his present life.

"I inherited Burtins from Mother as a provision…" Once again, his thoughts sank against a question neither of us could answer.

We ate the remainder of our breakfast in silence until he set down his utensils and said, "Now, what can I bring you from the village?"

"I have everything I need."

His gaze softened, and I didn't know why, other than it sent my heart into a plunge. I had everything I needed, but no, not everything I wanted. I looked down at my plate, unable to bear his kind regard. Was love merely a want? Or could it also be a need?

I was glad when he left the table, left me to myself. I shut my eyes against what I'd allowed myself to think and feel. This continual war within me had to stop. I let myself love him. Yes. There. I admit freely to myself. I was in love with Tobias Chinworth. Now, I might logically set this love aside, may God help me.

More important things were at play. Cecily's health, for one. I pushed my chair back and returned upstairs. Nothing like duty to put one's imagination and desires in place.

Chapter Five

Later in the afternoon, Tobias returned and subsequently sent Cummins packing. The caretaker had continued drinking through the night and was in no shape to form a coherent word. A stream of offenses poured from his mouth—of such that I had to cover Cecily's ears. I'd been watching the ordeal from the drawing-room window, none too amused to see the man dishonor Tobias in such a way.

The housekeeper had joined me. "Good riddance to that awful man. He's been naught but a pox on Burtins these five years," she harrumphed. "I've been after him to fix a leak in the kitchen for six months. Is it done, I ask you? Nay. Tis not." She folded her arms. "Carrying on at night with ne'er-do-wells and the like. Aye, once a man gets a spread of cards in his hands, he be hooked on the devil's game with no mind for anything else but strong drink and riches."

I wondered…"He doesn't look the sort to have enough money to gamble with in the first place."

Her eyes narrowed. "No, he don't." She shrugged. "Ah, well. Glad he's going. The next man better be the decent sort." She turned and smiled at Cecily. "I've some gingerbread coming out of the oven, sweetheart. Do you like it?"

Cecily nodded.

She did like gingerbread. With extra cream and berries atop. I wasn't sure the luxury would be afforded here. I hoped Cecily would adjust.

Tobias called to us from the front door. "Come, let me show you about the estate." The place between his brow wrinkled, but he smiled. A bit of strain was nothing compared to the shadows that had fallen upon him. The countryside was doing him only a little good thus far.

Cecily dashed through the door ahead of me, while Tobias tucked my hand on his arm. "Come now. You may admire my inheritance better from other views, I think."

His inheritance was no small thing. Most men had nothing left to them but the know-how of hard work. Some training, a bit of survival. That judgment that all men receive to plow their ground and work for their food.

However, his inheritance was shabby. Well-used and worn down to the bone. Twas true, if he would apply himself to the land's success, and its inhabitants, I believed it would render him a self-sufficient man that he desired to be. An investment of good returns.

"I'll warn you, Tessa," he said in a low voice, "the tenants are none too pleased with me and I don't blame them. I must somehow gain their trust if I'm to make headway here."

I had no clue as to how much they mistrusted Tobias, but I hoped it was derived from his absence and nothing else.

"First, let me take you to the ruins."

Ruins...my heart sped. How fascinating!

Burtins sat near a pair of steep hills around which we hiked. Twas beautiful. Green, rich. Homes dotted beyond and there—I could scarce believe it—were the ruins. Massive, tumbling remnants of a castle—and more.

"You see, Burtins is the new house." Tobias's lips quirked as he assessed my expression.

"New, eh?" I could not tear my eyes from the staggering sight.

Cecily began to run towards them.

Tobias reached for Cecily's arm. "Stay with us, Cecily. Do not run ahead."

Her eyes blinked with confusion. "Why?"

I glanced at the child, excitement emanating from her even while defiance set in her jaw. I'd never known a child to be so confined, yet so utterly spoiled at once. The tragedies had tempered her as they had Tobias. She was still terrified of much, but that didn't stop old habits. She would often try tactics to maneuver her way into attaining what she wanted. Samuel had used her. But we had to show her a different path—a better path that didn't end in so much destruction as it had before.

Tobias was afraid for her future. I had every hope in the world.

"What do you think?" He murmured.

Cecily folded her arms. "I think it is a place of knights and ladies."

"It was, long ago..."

We gazed at the sprawling ruins of stone upon stone, roofless structures, empty gate posts, the tall square of what once was the main living quarters. A small chapel with cathedral shaped windows. A flock of birds flew from the wide chimney that stood tall and unmoving. As though the great hearth that kept it warm, fed, and operating only needed firing up again to do the same.

Before we knew it, Cecily had defied her brother and was almost at the first gate.

"Cecily!" Tobias ran and I joined him, hardly able to keep up. She turned briefly, with a wild grin on her face, and entered her world of knights and ladies.

I shouted after her. "Cecily Chinworth, do stop!"

She was too taken with the ruins, her brother too little influence upon her stubborn nature.

I caught up to him just as he burst ahead and caught her shoulder. "When I tell you to stop, young lady, I expect obedience." He was none too pleased.

"Like Samuel? What will you give me in return?" The ruffle on her hem had turned upward as much as the pleasant start to her day.

I stopped before them, out of breath.

"What will I give you? Hmmm…" She tapped her dainty foot.

I couldn't believe he would dare negotiate with her after everything that had happened?

He knelt and took her hand. "I give you my protection from danger. You must halt, fair maiden, so that the uncovered wells do not swallow you whole and the rotting stair does not give way beneath you."

Her lips formed an o.

My resolve to set aside love failed. I would end up with a broken heart. There was no help for it.

He gave his sister his arm like a gentleman and led her forward—showing her this and that and the few dangerous places to stay away from.

I skirted one of the wells. Circled by a goodly pile of stone, the structure that would be above it had long disappeared. Burtins Hall was old. How much older was this place? Hundreds of years had flown. Hundreds of lives had passed through. And now we stood in the present, admiring its seeming romantic history. Twas a sobering thought, all told.

Cecily's mind was full of knights and ladies. Mine was full of humanity's continued scrape for survival. I turned to follow them, but my shoe caught something that clanked upon the flagstone.

Sunlight glinted upon it—a spoon? I bent to retrieve it. A silver spoon. As I picked it up, I spied another nearby. How strange. I was pretty certain these were no leavings from days gone by. Such would be long buried, tarnished, and trapped by nature.

Cecily also picked up something and squealed. She and Tobias ran towards me. "Look what we found!"

Tobias's eyes lit with pleasure. "Fancy finding a Roman coin in a place like this."

I lifted my finds. "How about two silver spoons?"

His jaw slackened.

"I suspect these belong to Burtins?"

He took one from my hand and inspected it. "Indeed so. Where did you find them?"

"By the well."

He looked in that direction. "I wonder if there are more."

We poked about the well and the surrounding area. Cecily squealed again. She discovered a butter knife and I another teaspoon. Tobias found nothing.

It didn't make sense to be so careless with valuable items. "Whoever it was that stole from Burtins must have been in a hurry."

Tobias put his hands on his hips. "Whoever it was had no need of salt, sugar, or silver. I believe they tossed the lot into this well."

"Do you think?"

He pointed from where he stood and I joined him. "There—the slanted top of the salt box. And a broken latch."

Sure enough, wedged against the stone was a remnant far out of place among these ruins. I'd heard of old women hiding valuables within salt boxes—or any old box that might be locked with a key. This one had clearly been busted open. We must have been thinking along the same lines.

Tobias lifted the smashed piece to inspect it. "Fredrickson doesn't keep salt in the salt box anymore. She called it an old, inconvenient tradition. Keeps it in a covered bowl."

"Silver has greater worth than salt. These might have been sold for profit. Not tossed like refuse." He took the spoons and tucked them into his coat pocket.

Cecily had tired of the ruins and made her way to the gates. We followed. "Do you think that Samuel was part of the theft?"

"Yes. But I cannot fathom why. He must have hidden something here without my knowledge and returned to retrieve it. But what was it? Why go through the trouble of making me think Uncle Mulls had died?"

"Perhaps we are to leave your brother's sins in the past. Whatever he did, it is done. It cannot be changed and mayhap there is nothing to be done about it. Thank God your uncle didn't die." One might live a good life with or without silver, though it is a loss.

"My brother's sins—whatever they may be—or my father's..." he took my hand and helped me up a steep section but did not let go, "have everything to do with the threat on my life. And more. I cannot explain it, but I feel that this is linked to everything else. And if I follow that link, I may find the babe. Just maybe."

I had not thought of that. Finding Samuel's lost babe had consumed him. But as much as he and our friends tried, the babe had not been discovered.

A threat and an attempt on Tobias' life had been made along with his uncle. His missing nephew, the stolen goods. Old sins and new... I prayed for clarity, for Tobias's sake. Discovering more about his brother might be too much to bear.

I grimaced. He'd already heard the worst of Samuel's intentions when Samuel planned to help his sick wife to the grave a few months ago. Tobias had been horrified at his sibling—and what he'd already done. Could he stand to discover more?

"I believe I must have another interview with my staff. And old Uncle. I feel there is something they aren't telling me."

We hiked back up the hills and rounded them, then meandered down a lane towards some cottages. Children of differing ages scampered about, but those of an age to work did so, whether hanging laundry on the line or hoeing the garden.

Cecily drew close to my side. She was unused to other children, and entirely unused to seeing them required to work.

"Do you know their names, Tobias?" I asked.

"Not a one of them." He swiped his handkerchief across his brow as the day had grown warm. He paused. "I shall rectify that on the morrow."

Some ten cottages or more were spread across the land. A row of three here, two there. Fields that ought to be tilled and filled with some growing produce lay empty, aside from the cottage gardens.

"Some of my tenants have uprooted to Manchester to attain a better living from the textile warehouses rather than scrape together a living at my pitiful estate."

"I can't believe it." The scene was glorious—but did his tenants truly starve? Enough to do that?

"The young do, at any rate. Uncle warned me this morning. I will lose the next generation if I don't do something about it now."

A few women peeked from the doorways, wondering at our arrival. A man approached. Tall and lanky, he removed his hat in my presence. "Good day to ye, Mr. Chinworth, sir." He nodded to me. "Miss."

Tobias acknowledged him. "How can I help you, Mister…"

"Mr. Ode, sir. If you please, I heard Old Cummins got the boot. This be true?"

Tobias nodded. "You heard right."

"I'm that relieved. The man brought all manner of gents 'round Burtins. Betimes they frighten the children."

"How so?"

"They come knockin' on doors, all drunken-like. Or try to catch a lass when she be out wandering the hills."

Alarm spread across his face. "It is worse than I thought."

"Aye, worse. We've had to keep an eagle eye on the lasses, mind ye."

I pulled Cecily away from the conversation and back towards Burtins. She needed to feel safe. Needed to *be* safe. So did Tobias. But since we arrived, Tobias had been met with issue after issue.

We needed peace and quiet, but most of all, safety. God, make it so.

We made it back to the kitchen for the gingerbread the housekeeper had promised. She didn't seem to mind that we'd invaded her space. She might be properly called a maid of all work as she seemed to fulfill the duties of cook and laundress as well. I hoped Tobias would provide extra hands for her.

"Have some tea, dears, and don't mind the mess on the table. Set ye down and have a bite. Supper will be at seven o'clock." Chopped vegetables and scraps littered her work space. Something lovely was roasting in the oven. The weather was warm, to be sure, but not too warm. The breezes that blew in through the open door soothed me.

Our first hours at Burtins had been strange and unexpected. I glanced at Cecily, her cheeks rosy from our exercise. I settled into a rocking chair and she the bench. She swiped at her eyes. Overly tired, I shouldn't wonder. "Would you like a lie down?"

She swallowed her tea and put a hand on my arm. "I haven't been a good child. I know it." Tears began to swim in her eyes. "But I want to be. I want to be like you, Tessa." Sobs began to shake her thin form. I pulled her into my arms and held her as she wept into my shoulder. I couldn't move. I held her and rocked her until she slept in my arms. My young prodigal needed so much love and attention. I blinked back my own tears.

The housekeeper swiped at her eyes at our emotional display and continued with her work. The hazy afternoon, the warmth, the long walk—how Cecily draped across my shoulder—lulled me as though I'd been rocked in a cradle. I fell asleep. I know not how long.

Sometime later, I felt Cecily being lifted from me. I blinked awake. Tobias. He winked at me before he carried Cecily to bed and returned to me a moment later.

I stood and stretched. It was most definitely later than seven o'clock. Twilight had descended, a few candles had been lit. I noted that the rustic work table had been set for supper for the servants and I had delayed their repast

Tobias held out his arm. "Shall we?"

He led me into the dining room where supper was indeed laid out. He seated me as I couldn't stop yawning.

"The journey has exhausted you both." He smiled. "I daresay you'll retire as soon as you sup."

"If I do, I shall read the night away. I feel quite energized."

Mrs. Fredrickson began to set covered dishes within reach. "I've another two servants coming on the morrow, Mr. Chinworth. Until then, I beg your patience."

"No need to apologize," Tobias said.

I stood and removed the covers. "I am quite capable of seeing us through supper." I nodded. "Do attend to your own needs."

She placed her hands on her hips. "This woman is a jewel, Master Chinworth. A jewel." She left the room swiftly while heat flooded my cheeks.

Tobias spoke, "I quite agree." I paused while serving his potatoes as his eyes captured mine. "I have great respect for you, Tessa."

I went back to work, serving the meat. Respect was good. I must latch onto that. Respect. Mayhap changing one regard for another would help me overcome my precarious feelings.

Chapter Six

The next few days passed amicably. Cecily and I cobbled together a new routine for ourselves. Twas good to put our minds to what we might do with these new and interesting surroundings. We took walks after breakfast. Applied ourselves to watercolors after lunch, and some light reading before her post-luncheon rest. The late afternoon included another turn about the countryside and a game of chess or some sort before tea. It was as much as her slight form and low energies could handle.

"How long will we stay here?" she asked, her bright eyes blinked in the sunlight. As much as she still needed to recover, a new bloom had set upon her cheeks.

I couldn't answer her exactly. Until Tobias deemed Mayfield safe? But were we even safe here? Theft and attempted murder were no small issues. Tobias and I both wondered why he'd not been contacted by the constable—or at least by Cummins. The man had been charged with taking care of Burtins, and sending all important communication to Tobias at Mayfield.

But Cummins proved to be a character not to be trusted. If he'd been in his cups and at cards too often, then not at all. I queried Tobias as we took a turn about the garden. "Why did not Mr. Mulls not find the time to inform you?"

"My uncle expected Cummins to do his job." Tobias shrugged. "The real issue is that this place is my sole responsibility. And I, alone, am responsible for everything that happened here."

Questions abounded. Mayhap my mind ran away with me. After the events last spring, I couldn't settle myself into any kind of true ease. I was ever on guard. I kept a dagger latched to my right leg, my small pistol within reach come eventide.

The man who had accosted Tobias in his bed-chamber had been all too real. More real than I'd experienced in the space of six years that separated my past from my present. It set my heart thumping betimes.

And the note? Did it only threaten the male Chinworths—or did it threaten the Chinworth daughter too? The idea put a sick feeling in my stomach. I imagined that it was Cecily's father whose actions caused our present troubles. The price was far too high. Samuel's additional actions had made life all the harder.

I gazed upon the verdant land, with Burtins' shabby structure—the ruins and cottages beyond. Tobias had spent hour upon hour assessing the ledgers that Cummins had left in a tangle, interviewing the cottagers of their needs, their present industry, and the fees that seemed to set them back financially—and yet the property could fain to do without.

This stunning piece of land needed his tending, finances needed balancing—so much to be done. Yet I believed a peaceful life might be made here. When, and if, and after...

Cecily took my hand and pulled me into a run; her shrieking glee broke me from my melancholy ponderings. She led me back to the ruins and paused. I could see the imagination building behind her eyes. Her lips lifted with a pure smile—nothing saucy about it. She was changing. She was beginning to hope.

I wondered if being away from her brothers, Samuel and Zachary, and sadly, her own father, along with the lessening of that nasty elixir, meant that she was no longer oppressed by her family's evils. No longer a captive of a belief, a mood, and the perceived malady that beset her as a smaller child. She'd been released from her tower to explore the true world, and not the one of her manipulative brother's making.

We'd wandered near the ruins, alight with the golden glow of summer. The place had a draw. I felt much like the young girl Cecily was—full of romance and longing.

"Come, Tessa." She waved me to her side. "Let us find more silver for Tobias."

I saw no reason to object. She exhibited new energy and wanted to do something for the brother that she'd had to learn to trust in such a short time.

"Remember not to go near the stairs. They aren't safe."

"You don't have to remind me, I remember the rules!"

She ran towards the well, though we'd searched thoroughly there first, we combed the area once again. After a time, we quite gave up. The rest of the silver likely lay in the mucky depths, waiting for a future treasure hunter to find it one hundred years hence. I laughed at the thought. In all probability, no one would think to look there in that strange future I'd thought up.

We meandered about the property that had been gracefully laid out and undoubtedly planned with a purpose. We approached a smaller structure with arched windows still standing along the sides.

"Tis the chapel, Cecily." Once a holy place, we entered the space where flagstone lay smooth and unmoved. There was a stone lift in the front—before it was an altar.

I imagined a good priest who presided over the former community, its livelihoods and shortcomings. I thought of the communion bread and wine offered here. The sacrifice that set us all free if we would but partake. I shut my eyes and offered a prayer of thanks, but as I did so, a groan emanated from behind the altar.

Cecily's hand went to her throat. I had not yet convinced her of the absence of ghosts. I placed a finger to my lips and reached for the dagger strapped to my leg and pulled the blade out. She startled at the sight. I would have to explain later. I gripped it fast and let the folds of my gown hide its presence. I tiptoed closer and peered over the side.

A man lay in a heap against the stone. Though I'd seen him but once, I knew it was Cummins. A very drunk Cummins. I moved closer to his head, and my heart stopped. He was bloodied. He'd been beaten.

Cecily tried to see what I'd found, but I caught her just in time.

"Let us find your brother. Tis naught but the old drunk man we met upon arrival."

"He smells terrible." She laughed. "Tobias should throw a bucket of water on him before he makes him leave Burtins. I threw a bucket of water on Samuel once."

"Did you now?" I made a half-hearted laugh at her comment; thankful she'd not seen the man's actual state. I could well believe Cecily had seen a few of her brothers wasted by drink. We hastened back to Burtins. Tobias would be very concerned.

He was.

"Cecily, will you stay with Mrs. Fredrickson and perchance learn to make bread—or something?"

Mrs. Fredrickson cast him a doubtful eye but waved the child over anyway.

Cecily hopped twice. "Might we make biscuits instead?"

At Cecily's pleading gaze, the older woman melted. "Indeed, we might! Put on this apron, lass."

Cecily ran back to me as I exited the kitchen. "I've always dreamt of baking." A hand pressed to her heart as though about to experience a wonder.

"Have you now?" I smiled.

Tobias bent and kissed the top of her head. "Mind and do exactly as she says."

Cecily gave him a curtsy and a gentle smile back. Respect he'd never received from her until this very moment.

Tobias gave her a bow in return, then tugged me quickly down the hall and pulled me into a quiet corner. My pulse pounded. "I hate to ask it of you, Tessa. I need you to accompany me to the ruined chapel. I'd ask the stable boy, but he is young yet. And I don't know if he can be trusted, given Cummin's behavior. He may have helped the man."

"I understand."

He grimaced as he retrieved a pistol from a cabinet near his desk and loaded it. "I acknowledge that I require your defensive skills as I might need of one of Joseph's men."

I was honored he did not discredit my ability. "No one was about the place, aside from Cummins. I don't believe we will be met with any sort of mischief." At least I hoped we wouldn't. "He was quite incapacitated."

"Let's go." He pushed through the door and I followed.

A few days ago, I'd shot a man and then promptly buckled beneath the emotional weight of what I'd had to do. And yet Tobias still trusted that I was strong enough to help him in this way? My heart shouldn't have warmed at that, but it did.

He took my hand as we fairly stumbled down the hill. "Did you see anyone or anything else odd?"

"Not at all. Cecily wanted to hunt for more silver. I never dreamed of finding the man behind the altar."

"I imagine not." We slowed by the entrance and made our way back to the chapel. I had my dagger ready once again, should I need it.

We stepped silently to the place where he lay and peered over the altar. But he was gone. "Where did he go? I promise you he was here."

Tobias bent to inspect the area. "Drops of blood on the flagstone. He can't have gone far" He spun around, glancing this way and that. But there was nowhere else to hide except behind the altar. He stepped softly to the back of the building and waved me to follow.

"I don't know how he was able to get up and run off so quickly. He was quite bloodied."

"Hmm. He might be crouching behind any one of these ruined structures."

A small stone tumbled close by. Then, a clanking sound.

"Indeed."

"I think old Cummins was merely playing dead." He stooped to pick up a silver butter knife and held it to me. "I think he must have had empty pockets on last night's gamble and came to retrieve some silver."

"A sound assessment. How curious he would know its whereabouts..."

"Isn't it, though? Perchance, he had dealings with Samuel. Or he was the one who shot at my uncle." Tobias cast a keen gaze among the ruins. "Come out, Cummins," Tobias shouted, "and let us talk. Let us help you tend your wounds."

No response.

"You are trespassing on my land, Cummins. I could see you in the gaol for this. Come out, do as I say." Still no answer. "These ruins are a maze. Finding him could prove a cat and mouse game." Tobias cocked his pistol. "A game I'm not in the mood to play." He shot into the air. Birds scattered.

I spoke quietly. "Tobias." He did not realize the mistake he'd just made.

"Hopefully that will scare him off."

"Far be it for me to correct you...but..."

He glanced down at his still-smoking pistol. "I've fired my only shot. Foolish of me."

I nodded. He had no way to reload. "The kit is in your study." I scanned the ruins, back and forth, high and low—as Joseph had taught me.

Tobias spoke in a low voice. "I daresay that you and I should walk back to Burtins without delay."

"He is gone," I spoke louder than needed. This time, I grabbed his hand and pulled him out of the ruins as fast as I could. Tobias didn't argue. If Cummins watched, he would think we'd given up. We crested the hill, but instead of turning down the lane back to Burtins, I stalled him just behind a rise. The place would be perfect for a picnic. And a lookout.

Tobias guessed at what I planned for us to do. "You are wise, Tessa. We will see which direction he runs when he leaves. Though I do wonder at my ancestors for building the castle at such a vulnerable position." He plucked the butter knife from my fingers. "However, we are left with a rather dull weapon..." He cocked a brow and we laughed until I showed him my dagger. "But of course you are prepared."

Our position was fortuitously out of sight of both the tenants and Burtins. We were entirely unseen and alone. I gulped at the thought as my betraying heart picked up pace. We sat in silence. We were used to being quiet together—so often we'd had to be so while attending Cecily. Our situation, being alone, was entirely inappropriate. But how good and right it felt!

I turned to face the object of our lookout. The ruins and bloodied Cummins.

We sat among the weeds for nearly an hour.

"There he is," Tobias murmured. "Crouching and limping—do you see him? He's heading west. Towards the village." He stood and helped me to my feet, but didn't let go of my hand.

A warm breeze slipped between us. His lips parted as if to say something, but he must have thought better of it. He released my hands and took a step back. "I am sorry—"

Once again, we had allowed ourselves to be alone together. Compromising in the eyes of most society. I filled the air with my own words, a little out of breath from the spark of his touch. "It could not be helped."

I wanted to tell him that he had no obligation towards me. I knew full well what we had done, what we'd done countless times because of a greater need. Cecily. Troubles. Life and death... I wouldn't count those things against him. He needed me and I would never expect him to pledge his troth to me solely based on these necessary indiscretions.

His demeanor changed, from thoughtful to something else. I couldn't put my finger on it. "There is much that cannot be helped." He continued to gaze upon me as if I might read his mind and heart, but alas, I could only know my own.

I couldn't help my heart either.

Chapter Seven

I tossed and turned the night through. But thanks be to God, Cecily did not. Since arriving several days ago, she'd taken a turn for the better. She was intrigued by Burtins and the grounds. The housekeeper had quite made a pet of her. More often than not, she begged to retreat to the kitchen, only to return to me in a few hours with smudges of flour upon her cheek and apron and a plateful of her attempts at biscuit making. Twas as if glory itself had opened up to the child.

Thankfully, Tobias had only encouraged her in this below-stairs activity, one not befitting a lady in the least. I smirked at the social rules. If society knew what being a lady really meant in old English, they would choose new, more polished titles. It simply meant: She who gives bread. To be a proper lady meant something far more precious than wearing silks and attending Almacks. Furthermore, a lady is one who performs a task, not out of duty but charity. A kind vicar once told me this upon my marriage. My husband had been of lower status, and I'd received a criticism from a woman after church on a Sunday. He'd heard and sought to encourage me. Not that I'd learnt to make bread—but I did understand his meaning.

While my marriage to a lower-class gentleman had been endorsed by the vicar, he could not have known how his words had impacted me over the years.

I slipped from bed early and quietly dressed for the day. I was surprised to see Mr. Mulls out of bed to join us for breakfast, this time, more properly attired.

He stood and bowed at my entry. "Good morning."

I curtsied.

"Mrs. Fredrickson tells me I was a bit brutish t'other day when you'd arrived." He grimaced. "I apologize. And to you, nephew."

"Uncle." Tobias nodded. "It is understandable after everything you've been through of late."

The old man's bushy brows rose as an odd smile lifted about his lips. "Right. Isn't every day a young lad pops in and tells one he ought to be dead." He laughed. "We all got our time. I'll have my real death notice someday." He tugged at his much-yellowed cravat. "But not today. Not yet."

I served myself some porridge and berries with fresh cream. A pot of steaming coffee waited on the table, beside the tea. I reached for the coffee.

Tobias' eyes lifted in surprise. "You take coffee?"

"I'd a troubled rest. Coffee will revive me."

"I'm sorry to hear it. I'm heading to the village this morning to have another meeting with the magistrate and constable." He tapped two letters on the table. "And I'm writing to Joseph for advice."

"Good idea."

"Tis a pity about young Samuel's death, nephew." Mr. Mulls filled his mouth with eggs and chewed. "Haven't seen him since he was sixteen, there about." He lifted a piece of toast to his lips. "The young ought not die. No, indeed."

So. He hadn't been aware of Samuel's visit. If he had been here at all—if he'd been the one to steal the silver as a ruse—if indeed Cecily had heard right. If she had not, then why had Samuel bribed her silence? No, it must be true. He'd come to Burtins in secret. Why hide his identity? Being a Chinworth, the firstborn to inherit the mighty Mayfield estate, he'd be welcomed incautiously. Especially here.

Tobias caught my train of thought with his own. "Whatever he came for would have been of benefit to himself. He did nothing unless it served himself."

Mr. Mulls poured more coffee. "What do you say, lad? Speaking ill of the dead?"

"I do. My brother left much ill in his wake."

Mr. Mulls offered a compassionate nod. "I'd such a brother. Mounting debts left from Manchester all the way to London. Then he popped off..." he snapped his fingers, "without so much as a by your leave. Buried in the graveyard where debts pursue no man. Well..." he pursed his lips, "I suppose there's the Big Debt, outside the mercy of God. Rather sobering, isn't it?"

Tobias chose to ignore the painful truth. "Tell me, Uncle, what do you think of my tenant, Mr. Ode?"

"Finer man never walked the face of the earth."

"Would he make a decent steward?"

"He'd be a far sight better than Cummins, I can tell you that. But I'll also tell you the man's got it in his hands to farm. You see what few crops fill the land? Those are his doing." He pointed his finger. "You should put him in charge of the farmable land. Entirely. The cottagers trust him. They look up to him. Get him on your side, the rest will follow." He nodded.

Tobias scribbled a note on some foolscap. "What stopped him from plowing the rest of the fields? If he is as good as you say?"

"Lad, I didn't take you for a dolt. But there you sit."

Tobias winced at his blunt words, as did I.

"You haven't figured it out?" His mouth quirked. "He scarcely had enough money to buy what seed he planted, mind. Precious little at that."

I watched Tobias squirm in his seat, becoming increasingly aware of his neglect. "I suppose it is too late to plant more?"

"You really know nothing of farming, do you?"

"I am the dolt you accuse me of being." Tobias opened his hands. "What else can I do to improve the tenant's lives?"

Mr. Mulls grinned widely. "Sheep. Get you a flock for the fields are quite overgrown and in sore need of grazing."

"Sheep." Tobias repeated. He pulled out his notebook again and penciled that in. "Got it."

Mr. Mulls thunked his thick finger onto the table. "But that's only the start. Your tenants must survive upon something until the land feeds them enough food and more besides."

"Indeed, they must. I'm beginning to think, Uncle, that you could be my steward."

"Nonsense. I'm only fit for kite making." His face lit as a sudden idea turned within his mind. "Do you think the young lass might desire a kite?"

The barest nod sent the man into raptures.

Mr. Mulls tossed his napkin to the table. "I shall create a kite like no other for the child." He swallowed a final gulp of tea and set his cup down in a clatter. "You have energized me, lad. I shall get directly to work!" He left the room, singing a song in deep baritone that echoed down the hall.

I couldn't help laughing. Kite making might well be as important as the rest.

Tobias smiled as he stood. "My uncle is a good sort." He snatched his notes from the table. "I must ride to the village. Please stay away from the ruins today. I'd rather you didn't run into Cummins again, no matter his state."

"Of course." I certainly didn't want to see that man again.

He swiped the letters from the table, pocketed the foolscap and left the room.

Cecily still slept, so I decided to write to Emma. I missed her companionship. The few years we'd had together had been sweet, though much confined. I hadn't minded being out of society's eye. The quiet life had suited me for the time.

I stepped into the drawing room and opened the secretary desk, hoping to find stationery, ink, and a quill. The little shelves within were empty but for an old lump of wax melted onto crackled leather of a writing pad. No one had written at this desk for a long time. I'd have to borrow from Tobias. I made my way to his small study at the other side of the house, down a narrow little hall where a cool draft snaked around my ankles, regardless of the day's heat.

I opened the door and stepped within. Such a mess! I'd never known Tobias to be so sloppy. Papers were scattered about the room, even the ink bottle had been tipped and spilled down the front of his desk and onto the rug. A chill prickled across my neck. Tobias wasn't sloppy. Someone had been here.

A sound shifted near the window drapery. I backed out of the room and shut the door, quickly retrieving my dagger. My pistol was upstairs, hidden from Cecily's sight. Too far away.

But one thing I could do—the heavy-looking hall table nearby might do to block the door. Whoever was inside wouldn't be able to get out except through the window. I shoved the thick piece as hard as I could in front of the door enough to jam the handle and ran outside, knocking into the young maid in training as I went.

I tossed a finger to my lips to keep her quiet.

Her eyes were wide. "Ye run like yer dress is afire, Miss!"

I retrieved my pistol, careful not to wake Cecily. She stirred just as I was leaving her room. I ran even faster out of doors, around Burtins, to the location of the study window. He'd have to leap to the ground as the study was at a higher level than the rest of the house. I stood behind a scratchy holly tree, prepping my pistol to fire. Twas short work. Joseph had trained me to do it quickly, within a minute.

By the time I finished, my hands shook. Could I shoot a man again? I thought of Cecily and the looming threat on Tobias's life. Mr. Mulls, too. I glanced at the study window, squinting as the sunlight grew brighter. No sign of movement. Fine. I'd wait. My shaking subsided as I took deep breaths. Courage welled up within me in the still, calming moment. Bravery was a choice, after all.

A scraping sounded—the window shifted, creaking outward. A man propped one leg out and another. He was about to land on his feet. And—

In a swift motion, he dropped to the ground on his knees, grunting. I aimed. "Don't move."

Cummins. He'd returned. He painfully grimaced, no doubt still injured from his beating. He spared me a glance and moved to leave. Oh no, not if I had the ability to stop him.

I steeled my voice. "I meant it, you are not to move. I know how to shoot."

He turned, his eyes now focusing on my pistol. He paled. "You wouldn't hurt a fly. Not your type." He bowed a clumsy bow. "You being a gentlewoman and all. I'll be on my way and won't be botherin' ye none. I was just here to fetch my belongings—what I left behind on accident. I been locked in, ye see."

He backed away, eyes on my weapon.

"I said you are not to move."

His chin jerked. "I bet ye never fired that afore."

I smiled. "A bet you'd lose, sorry to say." I tried a new tack. "I shot a man last week. Exactly in the shoulder. I daresay you wouldn't enjoy the same injury..."

He sneered. "You wouldn't!"

Tobias rounded the corner, his own pistol ready. I thought he'd left for the village. Thank God, he hadn't startled me into firing. "If I were you, I'd do as she says."

Tobias stepped closer. "Heard a ruckus in my study and fetched my pistol. Why were you in my study, Cummins?"

"I left something. Tis all. Don't know what this ridiculous bother is about."

"As I recall, your things were cleared out days ago. Under my watchful care."

His teeth clicked. "My mistake. Pardon."

Tobias tossed me a glance. "What shall we do with him, Tessa?"

"Does Burtins have a dungeon?"

A ghost of a look passed over Cummin's face.

"It's quite a cavernous place beneath. Tight in places. He might enjoy staying in the wine cellar. Which is mysteriously empty, by the way."

"Is it now?"

"Quite empty. Not a problem, since I'm only drinking tea or ale these days. But still. I believe a certain someone has been draining my stores."

Cummins stared blankly. No doubt the contents of the wine cellar had been beneficial to the gentlemen who had come to gamble the nights away.

I kept my focus on the scoundrel. I was sure he'd taken something. Else why upend a desk? "You might search him. See what he took from your office."

Cummin's face turned red. Ah. I was onto something.

Tobias kept his pistol pointed. "What did you take, Cummins?"

"Alright, alright." He swallowed as he reached into his vest.

"Slowly, man."

He pulled a folded stack of papers and let them fall to the ground.

"Interesting."

Cummins didn't say a word.

"Tell me what those papers contain that is so important you'd break into my study and steal them?"

He still didn't answer.

I cleared my throat. "Do you think he has more hidden on his person, Tobias?"

The man jolted. "I ain't disrobing in front of the lady."

Tobias smirked. "Let's have it then. All of it."

More was retrieved and tossed to the ground, including pound notes.

"Have a little hidey-hole in my study, did you?"

The man shrugged. "Every man has his secrets." His eyelids lowered to a squint. "I bet you do too, Tobias Chinworth. I've heard stories, mind ye."

Tobias was unfazed by the threat. "Redemption has a way of setting a man straight."

"You sound like a vicar."

"I hope that I do."

"Gone religious. That's for women, man."

Mr. Mulls came limping slowly around the corner. "I thought you might need some string. To tie him." The rope that hung from his grip was no kite string but strong hemp.

"Good thinking, Uncle." He nodded to me. "Keep your aim, Tessa. I will tie him." He handed his pistol to Mr. Mulls, whose hold was a bit shaky.

My arm began to ache even as relief coursed through me. Thank God, I'd not had to deal with the situation alone.

"Don't tell me that woman can shoot?"

Tobias laughed. "She wasn't lying."

Cummins offered me a cold stare and a curse. "Bluestocking," he spat.

I aimed at his foot as a retort fell from my lips. "Call me that again, and I will put a hole in *your* stocking."

Tobias jerked the man's vest open. "I rather like bluestockings. Ones that shoot, at any rate."

"Humph." Dried blood caked around his hairline and he sported a bright purple eye; his breathing was tight and hitched. Broken ribs, mayhap. Why had he tried to break in when he obviously needed convalescing?

"What have we here? More that belongs to Burtins I believe." Tobias tossed a salad fork and three sugar spoons to the pile. "You could be hung for this."

Cummins was quiet and immobile.

A few thoughts ran through my mind. Tobias's own father awaited trial. This might also be his fate. The next thought was—for one so poor and petty as Cummins, the trial would be far too swift. His execution would silence any information that might be of import to Tobias.

"You did say you had an adequate wine cellar to keep him?"

He offered me a slow nod, trying to guess my thoughts.

"Free room and board—" I took a risk. Would Tobias be angry? "And perhaps your troubles will not be as...final as expected."

He swallowed. "She in charge of Burtins?"

Tobias' brows rose. "Take the offer or swing from a noose."

He jerked a nod. "Alright."

Mr. Mulls wasn't entirely in tune with my idea. "What? Are you going to keep him here? You'll naught get a thing out of him, Tobias. You'll be a goose sitting on a rotten egg."

"You may be right. If he goes rotten, the constable can have him. For now, we'll give him a chance to make the right choice."

Tobias piled up the stolen items and handed them to Mr. Mulls. Then, we took him, with Tobias leading and my pistol ready.

Minutes later, Cummins under lock and key, Tobias gathered the staff to explain. "The constable will be informed in due time. You have no need to worry, Cummins isn't armed, but he is under lock and key. Do not talk to him, or you will lose your position. Am I clear?" A chorus of yeses and agreements sounded. But I knew the way of things, a word whispered here and there, gossip could wend its way into the village and beyond. But to whose detriment?

After the small staff was dismissed, Tobias took the stolen bundle from Mr. Mulls to the dining room and spread it out.

"Burtins is grossly understaffed. I cannot be everywhere at once." He took a handkerchief from his pocket and swiped his brow. "I still need to ride to the village and—"

I laid my hand on his arm. "First things first."

"You are right. I will get everything done—one thing at a time. Now—I must know. What were *you* doing in my study?"

A stone sank into my stomach. Was that a sliver of mistrust? "The secretary was empty of letter-writing paper supplies. I'd hoped to write to Emma..."

He shifted and took a breath. I looked away from him, through the window that let the sun brighten the room so thoroughly. I'd warned myself countless times of becoming too attached. My feelings were a nuisance. An outright disruption to any use I might be to him.

He placed a hand on each of my shoulders and turned me back to him. "Tessa. Did you think I questioned your honesty?"

He stood so close to me, my heart thrummed. "I—" I couldn't answer him. Didn't he?

"You must understand," his tone urged, "I was terrified when I realized that you had him cornered—and would attempt to capture him alone. Please never try to hold a man single-handedly. If something ever happened to you, I'd never forgive myself."

I swallowed and eked out a singular fact. "I only thought of Cecily and..." *You. I thought of you.* He'd endured too much. A lump formed in my throat. The depths of his brown eyes pulled me in. The genuine care. The warmth. Dare I hope?

He blinked slowly. "While I depend on your skills and must utilize them at times, I will be honest. When that man attacked me in my chamber at Mayfield, I had to watch you bring him to his knees, without my help. You were brilliant but I was undone. I trust your ability, yet I fear harm to your person."

Same as I. His eyes begged me to believe his words, not just the truth of them but something more. What would it be like? To be loved by such a man? I wanted to lean into it, this aura that hung between us. Give in to it. Fear snaked in. If I did, everything would change. I would have to leave and never show my face at Mayfield or Burtins again.

Mayhap he realized what he was doing. We shouldn't—he shouldn't stand so close...Tobias released his gentle but firm hold, his hands hanging limp at his side. But he did not release his eyes from mine. They captured me, held me as I'd never been held before. My heart, my heart was a captive, and I didn't want to be set free. My breath hitched as he stepped closer. Warmth spread across my chest that had nothing to do with the warmth of the day. His hand came beneath my elbow and stalled. He sought to calm me. That was all...

Laughter—someone was laughing. I blinked, aware. Was it Cecily? In the kitchen. We both shifted at the joyful sound. I moved a few steps back while he glanced at the stolen papers on the table. I knew we must not pursue what I felt—I must not pursue what I felt. It was not my occupation. Wasn't it? Questions and self-doubt began to plague me.

He cleared his throat, rummaging through the papers. "What did Cummins need from my study—let's take a look. Mostly pound notes. I did not bring them, they aren't mine. Ah, what's this?"

What we discovered plunged me into a deeper conundrum that had naught to do with my heart.

"A list of names. Samuel's is here." He stilled, glanced at me with concern. "As is this gentleman, six years gone." He pointed and looked at me. There, in black and white, was my dead husband's name. Patrick Audlington.

A black spot was placed beside it. Samuel's and Zachary's names were there too, but had been crossed out in a nasty slash. Seeing Patrick listed among the others made it all the stranger! The room grew hot. My palms broke out in a sweat. Tobias's name was also listed. Underlined, little ink taps at the place. As though the scribe had been thinking. Thinking about something with Tobias. To live or die? Or... pay?

If markings were any indicator, whoever made this list intended death. I needed air. I pulled my handkerchief from my pocket and began to pat away perspiration. I was going to be sick.

Chapter Eight

"Sit down, Tessa. You look faint."

I did as told.

Tobias opened the door to the kitchen and shouted. "Tea, Fredrickson! Posthaste."

"Right, sir. But a moment," the woman's voice filtered down the hall.

How could Tobias be so composed? "Are you not stunned to see your name listed?"

"At this point? No. I am not. I'm not surprised by anything anymore. Father and Samuel clearly had some doings here, what exactly?"

"Why is your name on that list?" I wanted to know.

"Because I'm a Chinworth, why else?"

Mrs. Fredrickson brought in the tea and set it beside the pile of evidence.

I moved to pour, but Tobias stayed me with his hand. "No, let me." He filled a teacup, added cream, and set it before me. "Drink up. You need steadying."

"Is being a Chinworth so dangerous?"

"I think we know the answer to that. But here, I am more concerned that Audlington's name is there." He sent me a significant look. "I begin to think dear cousin Joseph was right to advise a new surname for you."

Why was Patrick's name on the list too? He was long gone. Why was there a list at all? I recalled how Tobias reacted when he learned my dead husband's name. He'd recognized it. A coincidence? A mere memory from the newspapers? Or was there a connection between them?

My husband had been innocent, so I thought. Samuel was certainly not. Tobias had stepped away from doing his father's bidding—but how much had he done for him? And had he been aware of what he had been doing? Or the ramifications?

I swallowed more tea as Tobias shuffled through the other papers and found something else of interest. "A list of items. Specifically, weapons." He set it down and paced away from the table. "I brought you and Cecily here to get away from danger. Seems impossible to escape it."

"What have you—or anyone else on this list to do with weapons?"

"Tessa, I wish I knew." He loosened his cravat. "I wonder why Cummins returned here when he ought to be attended by a physician?"

I set my cup down and folded my hands. Tobias was right. Danger lurked, even here. "He himself is under a threat."

"I believe you are right. I need to speak with my father. If he would talk." Resolution sparked in his eyes. "I need to know why he was so dead-set on my leaving Mayfield to come here. I fear he plans something even from his cell."

"Surely not." Old Mr. Chinworth been a much grieved and broken man upon his return after Samuel's death. "At least I hope not."

"Father has an unfortunate habit of doing wrong to make a right. While he has seemed penitent enough, old habits die hard."

"What will you do?"

"I need time to think. Ready yourself and Cecily for a trip to the village. I dare not let either of you out of my sight. Not today."

"As you wish."

I rose, attended Cecily, and tied on our straw bonnets. "You must be so curious to see the village." I encouraged her with a smile I managed to conjure. It was hard to be bright and positive after such a morning, and such foreboding findings.

Cecily was reluctant. "I want to be in the kitchen with Mrs. Fredrickson, please. May I?"

"You may just as soon as we return from the village. Your brother most particularly wants to show it to you."

A flash of her old impatience swept across her face. "Why? Probably just another poky old village like Butterton."

"Now, Cecily. Butterton isn't pokey, it is quite lovely and you know it." Indeed, it was a charming refuge from the hustle and bustle of Town.

She sighed, disappointed.

"Go ask Mrs. Fredrickson if she requires anything." Cecily did as bid and returned with a smile and a list.

I didn't have the heart to tell her that Tobias worried for our safety. By the time we were ready, the horses had been attached to the small hack, and we were on our way.

Tobias had much business to attend to. Letters to post, inquiries concerning the sheep he'd been advised to purchase. A doctor to fetch, along with the local magistrate. Tobias felt it necessary to stay above the law no matter what.

I blinked at his design slowly. There were times when the law wasn't precisely upstanding. This was a cold, hard fact. Could we trust the local magistrate? Was he law-abiding? While I had wondered about a swift execution regarding so gross a theft—and had used such imaginings as a threat to Cummins, sometimes connections ran deeper and darker than a judgment. Remembering the things that had happened to Joseph gave me pause. Did the men fraternize? Gamble and get drunk together?

But Tobias was set in the matter. I couldn't change his mind, even if only for a few days. While he intended to keep Cummins under lock and key at Burtins, he would inform the proper authority. He refused to follow in Samuel's and his father's footsteps.

Cecily and I waited in a small parlor while Tobias held conference with the man. We would have liked to wander the village on our own, but he refused us that freedom, too. Fear laced his eyes once again. He was so tired. Tired of everything. He didn't trust us alone at Burtins or in the village. If I were honest with myself, it felt good that someone cared enough about me to protect me for a change. I didn't have to rely only on myself.

Cecily leaned her head against my shoulder and took my hand. What she said next was a spark that set my face aflame. "I know you love my brother." She patted my hand, looking up at me with her pale blue eyes. "I won't tell him. I hope he loves you back so I don't have to lose you." Her voice quivered. "I don't want you to leave me." She hid her face.

A lump rose in my throat. "Do not worry, my dear. I don't plan on going anywhere." Not for a long time. I couldn't make promises, no matter how much I wanted to. One couldn't force another to love. I thought back to the events of the morning—what had I sensed in him? Had I really sensed his regard, even passion? Or did I confuse the matter due to the strength of my own feelings?

I put my thoughts aside and focused on my young charge. "What do you plan to cook with Mrs. Fredrickson?"

"She promised, if I were to acquire a cake of raisins, that we might make rock cakes." Her voice lifted at the thought. "I never knew lower-class work would be gratifying."

I gave her a nudge. "Work is always gratifying, regardless of class. We are created to work. All of us. Even the richest man on earth is made for it."

Her eyes widened. "I heard Tobias talk to one of the tenants about helping with a roof." She laughed. "I can't imagine him sweating like a common laborer in naught but shirtsleeves."

Did he plan to personally invest in his tenants' lives this way? Posh. The fact made me care for him all the more. "It will be good for him."

She shrugged. "I suppose if I can enjoy kitchen work, he is allowed his pleasures."

"Indeed." I laughed.

Tobias stepped from the magistrate's office, the man following him. "Let me know when I need to fetch him. Just send word."

"I thank you." Tobias gave us a slight bow. "Ladies? If you will. We are well past luncheon, but Mr. Tanner assures us the local inn will serve us well. Shall we?"

We made our way down the cobbled street and passed by a draper's shop, a book shop, a solicitor's office, and a row of houses next to the inn that stood tall and proud. For a small village, it was remarkably tidy and well-maintained.

"I hear it is owned by Lord Bennington—his estate lies north of here. He owns the entire village, for that matter." He opened the door for us, and we stepped in.

I'd never heard of him. I blinked in the sudden shadows of the candle-lit dining room and looked around, right to left, front to back. As Joseph had taught me, I should not fear my surroundings or be suspicious of them, but *instead know them*. As philosopher Francis Bacon once said, "knowledge is power." Or rather, forewarned is forearmed if need be.

But what I saw weakened me, tested my knowledge. Shocked me, body and soul. I could not think, could not comprehend the sight before me. My dead husband. He was here. Sitting at a table with another man, a mug of ale gripped in his hands. I'd know him anywhere. Air flew from my lungs. I couldn't breathe.

"Tessa?" Tobias's voice sounded far away.

I grew hot, my head buzzed. Patrick was supposed to be dead. I'd seen his body. I'd identified him at the cold morgue—I—Patrick looked at me and resumed his conversation. He didn't know me. I didn't understand...what was happening? Patrick was dead. These six years, cold in his grave, his soul in the presence of God.

"Tessa..." I heard my name as my vision grew fuzzy. I buckled and knew nothing.

A sharp tang cleared my senses. I blinked, my heart pounding. Smelling salts followed by the biting scent of onions. "There she is, wake up, dear." An older woman in a ruffled day cap hovered before me. "There you are, sir, your lady has recovered."

I sat up, a hard settee beneath me. Cecily clung to my legs, weeping. Tobias knelt beside her, a hand at her back. "Cecily, dear." My heart still pounded, and my mouth had grown quite dry. Patrick was in the other room. "I am alright." I tried to smile. "I just need a bite of luncheon."

Cecily moved closer and wrapped her arms around me. "No more weeping, dear." I had thought my tears long over. Indeed, they threatened to spill down my present life as ferocious as a tidal wave.

If Patrick were alive, then I would still be married. I could not, must not love the man that stood before me, gazing upon me with such tenderness in his eyes. Nay, I must close it off. But why had not Patrick come forward when he saw me? All was confusion. In the days after Patrick supposedly died, I'd begged God to wake him, to send him back to me like Lazarus, raised. I ought to be happy, but I felt plunged into a kind of darkness.

The old woman pulled Cecily away from my neck. "If you please, miss, might I take the young lass to wash her face? I'll return her directly." Her tone was gentle and kind, like Mrs. Fredrickson. Cecily agreed, thank God.

I had to tell Tobias. I had to tell him the truth immediately.

I swung my feet from the settee to the floor, and he sat beside me.

"What did you see, Tessa? What is wrong?" His arm came around my shoulder. "I know you saw something awful, but I can't understand what for the life of me." His gaze became urgent. "If I am to be your protector, you must speak." He shifted his arm. "Wait. Is it one of the men who harmed you in the past?" His fingers clenched into a fist.

How I longed for his affection, his touch. His protection. Tears spilled from my eyes. I eeked out a whisper. "My husband. Sits in the dining room."

He stiffened. "What are you talking about? Your husband is dead."

"So I thought."

"How is it possible?"

"I do not know." I pleaded with him. "I saw his body, Tobias. He was dead. The constable made me look at him, though I desired it not." I swiped at my eyes. "He was dead. Well and truly. I don't know how...I..." Tears clogged my throat. For the trauma and grief I'd endured. For the love with Tobias I'd never experience. How was it going to be? Could I love my husband again?

Did he want me back? Six years. Six long years had gone by and he'd not returned to me. Why? Was I to be the abandoned wife?

Tobias took both hands in mine and held tight. "To be clear: you saw Patrick Audlington in the dining room, sitting at a table."

"Yes."

"Are you certain?"

The same eyes, the same nose, the same curve to his lips... was it him? "I..."

He stood and pulled me up. "We must face him, Tessa. Come."

"Tobias, he looked at me. He looked at me and showed no recognition." Doubts began to rise. Had my mind played tricks upon me? Had these stressful events, nay, even seeing his name inked so clearly on the list along with some living, some dead, wreaked havoc on my imagination? "Mayhap I am for the asylum." I shook my head. "I do not know."

Tobias tucked a stray strand of hair behind my ear. "There is no madness about you, love."

Love... how could he call me that—if he knew that Patrick was sitting in the next room?

My limbs were weak as I allowed Tobias to take me back to the dining room, back to my fate—or my future? Perchance my fury if I were truly abandoned. I'd prayed, hadn't I? God would give me the grace to bear this pain. I wouldn't be alone. I clung to that single promise.

"Take me to him, Tessa," Tobias whispered in my ear.

We rose and reentered the dining room. Faces turned toward me—had I caused much commotion? There. There he was. He also looked my way again, then resumed his luncheon. How? How could he? Tears smarted. I took another step, then another.

Tobias whispered. "Is that him? On the left?"

I gave a nod. We were almost at his table. The two men faced us, confused. Upon closer look, my certainty melted. He was Patrick—but he wasn't. I didn't know. Perhaps time had erased some of my memory of him.

Tobias offered a bow, and the men rose from the chairs. He addressed my ghost-husband first. "Are you Patrick Audlington?"

"Who is asking?" His eyes narrowed. He had yet to recognize me. Inconceivable.

"Chinworth."

He swallowed and finally gave me another glance, but it was brief. Still, nothing. He returned his attention to Tobias. "Have we business, sir?" The men lowered back into their chairs.

There was a mole beneath his chin. Patrick didn't have a mole. *Patrick didn't have a mole...*

"We do if your name is Patrick Audlington."

The man shrugged. "That is what they call me."

His left ear had an odd little point. Patrick had not. This man was not my husband. Relief and dread both flooded through me. I tugged Tobias's sleeve. Something was terribly wrong. How can a man be so like my deceased husband? Patrick had no brothers. And yet, this man had the same name. A name I'd had to bury in the past to keep evil at bay.

What did he play at?

Tobias ignored my signal, so I spoke up. "You are most certainly *not* Patrick Audlington."

"And who are you?" The man rejoined.

I gained strength. "Miss Smith."

"I don't know what it is to you, *Miss Smith*, but my friend and I would like to continue our business at hand. Please excuse us."

His voice was different, too. Nothing like the man I'd married. Why had I thought he was? But there remained his name.

Tobias plunged ahead. "Would appear you've taken a name you do not own."

The man sitting opposite him tossed his napkin to the table. "What do they talk of, Audlington? He said you were on the up and up."

The imposter shrugged. "Many men enjoy the same name."

Tobias shook his head. "Maybe the same name, but not the same name and similar features. You play at something. I believe you owe it to the world to be honest. Tell your business partner here what your true name is. Be an honest man, or you will regret it in more ways than one."

A wave of caution flared. Tobias's personal walk down the redemption road may have taken him too far. He valued honesty above everything these days. I wondered at the wisdom of our confrontation. Maybe we needed to back off. Seek answers another way.

The imposter's eyes flashed, and he swore. He stood, knocking his chair behind him, and threw a few coins onto the table. He bounded from the inn. Tobias chased him before I could stop him. The other man followed, causing no short of a ruckus among the inn's patrons.

I was about to follow them through the door when the kind innkeeper's wife brought Cecily to me. I could in no way take Cecily along. So we sat, helpless, waiting.

What on earth had just transpired? I scarcely knew. I did know that truth has a way of catching up to a man to hold him accountable, no matter how far he ran. Lies simply aren't ingestible. None can keep one down for long, if one does, well, the poison of it takes over. Is that not what was wrong with the world? A lie and a greedy trust in it?

The kind innkeeper brought us tea and stew. I hated waiting. But I also hated not knowing why a man had stolen my dead husband's name and looks. How was that even possible?

"Where is my brother?" Cecily asked.

"Finishing some...business." What had I said about lies? I couldn't tell her exactly. It was some business of a sort. I hardly knew how to explain.

Cecily took a swallow of her tea. "I know something is up. I'm not stupid, but I don't have to know what it's about." She winked.

I agreed with her. "You are correct. Something is up. Something rather confusing. I pray Tobias is able to sort it out directly."

As I sipped my tea and tried to eat the stew, I wondered. Was this the Patrick Audlington the same one written on the list? The one with the black dot by his name? The men who were dead had been crossed out. And Patrick's, oddly, had not been. This must be the case. Yet a sense of unease nagged.

It's a strange emotion to be relieved that my husband was still in his grave. Never did I expect to think thus. We waited for mere minutes before Tobias returned, his cravat askew and his hat rather absent. He took a chair and was promptly served.

He lifted the pewter mug took a deep drink of ale. He set it down and gave me a pointed look. "Gone."

"And the other gentleman?"

"A man of business, supposedly in the market for implements." He shook his head. "Refused to give me his name. At least, he ignored my request with a clutter of words. The man was clearly frustrated to be so inconvenienced."

"Implements? What kind?"

"He didn't say, but I do have my suspicions."

"The list of items we found on Cummins?"

"Precisely."

I shook my head at the entire conundrum, outright dizzied by it.

He reached across the table and took my hand. "I am sorry for your distress. It must have been quite a shock to see him." He squeezed then let go.

One of the kitchen maids brought his stew and a fresh pot of tea.

"Whoever this Patrick is, he paid for his luncheon. He might have easily run and not been so..."

Tobias paused. "Honest?"

"Yes. Don't you find it strange?"

"Perhaps he hadn't yet decided his course of action. He could have simply run and left without paying if he was able to disappear so easily." Tobias took a bite of stew. "Well noted, Tessa. But it may be irrelevant. He can't be up to anything good."

I took a bite of bread as another thought formed.

Tobias hurried us. "Come, let us finish here. The doctor waits at the livery.

Chapter Nine

When we returned to Burtins, I settled Cecily down for a short nap before tea, despite her insistence that she needed no rest. I could see the old weariness about her eyes. "Just for an hour, dear. I'll see that Mrs. Fredrickson remembers her promise about rock cakes."

That seemed to calm her, and she was asleep within a few minutes.

I came downstairs just as Tobias entered the side door with the doctor. "Since Cummins is aptly afraid of you, Tessa, come down to the cellar with us—here—hold my pistol, thank you."

I gripped the weighty weapon firmly, smirking at the doctor's surprised expression.

The doctor nervously cleared his throat. "I suppose you are a woman of—of—" He stuttered around, unsure of how to finish the statement he was trying to make, without giving offense, I sensed.

Tobias finished for him. "Substance and quality with the ability to defend herself as the occasion arises."

The doctor's expression remained stunned. "Miss." He bowed. "I hope the occasion does not arise. Women do not generally see such, or participate in such shocking episodes..."

I couldn't let the fallacy alone. "You are a doctor. I believe you have seen your fair share of abuses women do unfortunately endure, of episodes they most certainly never wanted to play a part in."

He turned a shade of red. I'd hit my mark, bullseye. He made no other rejoinder than another bow, now realizing that I was no ignorant gentlewoman whose head was in the ballroom or the perpetual teacups while plotting a marriage. I'd experienced life as it truly was, however unconventionally shocking.

I understood that while many women were indeed protected, most were not. After helping Emmaline learn to defend herself last spring, to some degree, there grew within me a passion for unprotected women that had since blossomed. I could do more than merely protect myself. I glanced at Tobias. I could protect those I loved.

I would not, must not swoon again. Never again. I steeled myself against weakness. Tobias needed to trust my ability. I needed to trust it also.

We followed Tobias down the deep, cool steps to the wine cellar, the keys jangling as the door was unlocked. I held his pistol to aim, lest the man think he could overpower us. Oft there was naught more fierce than a wounded animal, or man.

"Stand back from the door, Cummins. I have the doctor; he is here to help you." Tobias pushed it open.

"Cummins?" Tobias shone the chamberstick about the room. Twas empty. "Where is he? Who let him out?"

I looked behind us, towards the storage room. We searched around a stack of old, rickety crates and a few empty barrels. I skirted behind a bin of potatoes and onions. "He isn't here."

Tobias's shoulders slumped. "How could this happen? I gave strict instructions!"

We climbed the steps back to the kitchen, where Tobias gave swift orders to gather all of his staff.

I had not observed Tobias this angry since Samuel killed Zachary in his drunken stupor. Quiet and seething, he paced.

The young doctor sat in the corner nearest the doorway, mildly amused by the dramatic turn his day had taken, no doubt. Would he scribble the tale in his journals later of the pistol-wielding woman?

Mrs. Fredrickson wrung her hands. The new, young maid looked down at the flagstone floor. The stable boy stood his ground. "I hate the man, why should I help him? He beat me, didn't he? I'm glad he's off so he can't no more."

Tobias placed a hand on the boy's shoulder. "I am sorry to hear it. It should never have happened to you. I assure you that such will not again. You may go attend your duties." The boy ran from the room, anxious to feed the horses.

Mr. Mulls sat and grumbled. "I was making Cecily's kite. I looked from the window several times but didn't see man or beast scampering about the hills."

"How did he escape?"

Tobias shook his head. "I cannot figure it out. The door was locked, and the room was empty. 'Tis as though he vanished."

"If no one set him free, then I believe you must check the old wine cellar for a different way out."

"I will check again. Staff, you are dismissed." He turned to the young doctor. "I will loan you a horse. You must be anxious to return to the village."

The doctor bowed. "I thank you. Do send for me if any other need arises. Oh, perhaps it will help you to know that Cummins is a known character. I've heard rumors about him among the villagers."

"What kind of rumors?"

"That he is a pickpocket, of the worst sort. Though it has been difficult to prove."

"I should have returned to Burtins sooner." Tobias folded his arms.

I wasn't surprised—not after seeing him with Burtins's silver. But if the doctor had heard the rumors, then the magistrate would have? Surely? In a village this size would be unavoidable. Wouldn't someone have accused him, turned him in to the law by now?

Tobias and I made our way back down the cellar steps. We pressed and pushed against the aged stone, checked the cold, damp floor. "It appears that my property was on its way to becoming a gaming den of thieves."

I thought of the list Cummins had stolen from Tobias's study, the names on them, the weapons list—everything we had to go on. "I do believe it a den, mayhap much of more than thievery."

Tobias closed his eyes and leaned against the back of the cool cellar wall. His mind must be as overwhelmed as mine. Too much had happened already. Too much was happening now.

"Are you alright?" I moved closer.

His eyes blinked open. "I was praying for help." A soft smile rose. "I simply cannot figure out how he escaped."

"Unless..." I lifted my chamber stick and looked up. He did, too. "Ah."

We had our answer. The candle glow revealed a giant, gaping hole in the ceiling, showing rugged floor joists and a large enough path for the man to crawl through. A bit of rope dangled from it. Tobias pulled and found it to be well anchored, with thick knots for climbing.

"Only the most determined man could do it," I said.

"Likely a man who has done it many times before." Tobias gave it a try and slid down unsuccessfully. "He was helped. Had to be."

"But who would come to his aid? He was not liked among your staff, that much was clear." They seemed entirely innocent.

Tobias snatched his chamberstick and pulled me from the room, locking it tight. We went upstairs to the third floor. "I didn't want to be overheard lest he be hiding like a rat within the walls. I will search the crawl space tonight."

"Shouldn't you have help? Please don't go alone. Perhaps I can be of assistance."

He took the chamberstick from my hands and blew out the flame. "You shan't go, Tessa. I will be crawling through a hole that leads who knows where. It will be dirty with a century of grime. Full of spiders, like as not." His nose wrinkled. "No help for it."

The thought wasn't at all inspiring. However, if Cummins were able to wiggle through, it would be easy for anyone. "Can you not call for the magistrate first?"

"Not enough time. He might escape by the time he arrived."

"You are right." I shrugged. "I guess that leaves me."

He put his hands on his hips and cocked his chin. "*Miss Smith*. You will stay at Cecily's side as she is of great import to the Chinworth family." His chin dipped. "Please. I trust you to protect her."

I noted the seriousness of the situation. The true nature of my position. "This I will do. But know that I will worry over you while you are gone. I wish you would get help." I sounded very much like a wife, and it stabbed my heart.

"I shall. I wonder if Mr. Ode is up for an adventure. Or the stable boy? He will do as I bid. I've half a mind to send the lad to Joseph for training. I am incensed to know that Cummins had been beating him. It is unconscionable."

"It is. I think that's an amiable idea." I tried to smile. "I will be waiting up for you."

He bowed, then spoke in a soft tone that was my undoing. "I thank you, Tessa, once again. For everything." His eyes seared me to the soul. Would it ever be so? He leaned over me, and I burned. I couldn't step away from him, nor could I speak. He shifted, then bent and kissed my forehead. I sucked in air at the press of warmth—of affection. But before either of us could react, he turned and sped away. His action left me breathless. Had it been as though he kissed his sister? Was it a momentary thoughtlessness? It must have been.

His overly tired mind wasn't thinking.

I wandered to my room, a hand over my heart. Could it take much more? I did not know. I did not want to be his sister.

When Cecily awoke, we ate a solitary supper in the dining room and played a round of cards, a bit challenging due to being only two players. Then she scampered off to Mrs. Fredrickson for the promised baking, and I spent time doing nothing but gazing from a rather warbled window onto a distorted landscape. If only we might see clearly...

My heart was raw. On this day, I'd seen my husband alive—or so I thought. It sent me spiraling into such fear as I'd never known. The fear of losing Tobias, not Patrick. The fear of never being able to truly love him and belong to him. I could not go back in time. I would not change my story as hard as parts of it had been. I squeezed my eyes shut and rubbed the dull headache that began behind my eyes.

My heart had gone far beyond a mere admission that I loved him. I was dedicated to him. His life, his well-being. It was heavy to carry these feelings alone. I hardly even know how they started.

I'd been a companion to Emmaline sent to help her choose a mate between three brothers. Without her knowledge, I'd been positioned for the past two years by Joseph, who desired to see us both safe. When we left the outskirts of London for the countryside of Butterton, I thought my job would be a simple one. Emma was no fool. It didn't take much to influence her away from the Chinworth gentlemen. She'd chosen none of them from the start, believing Joseph's warnings. Yet I could not protect my own heart from such demise. My heart had chosen a Chinworth, for better or worse.

What do I do with my love, God? What? I begged my Creator for help. No answer came but for a stillness. I must wait. For that, I would need strength.

When it was time to attend Cecily, she donned her nightgown and we read a novel, each taking turns. It was hard to focus, so occupied were my thoughts. I must have gone quiet when it was my turn to read. Cecily's hand slipped into mine.

"You don't have to read any more, Tessa. I'm tired. I'm ready to go to sleep."

I sang her an old song of medieval days and set her dreams to knights and ladies at the old castle ruins. Then I left the room and sank onto the steps. Waiting for him.

Tobias hadn't told me of his continued plans to snake through the opening in the crawl space in the cellar. I hoped he would find me—at least inform me when he was about to do so. He was serious when he said he didn't want me to follow, that I was to see to Cecily's protection. I didn't blame him. I wanted to be with her.

I nodded off to sleep a few times, finding myself leaning against the cold, hard stone wall along the stairs. I rose and arched my stiff back. I needed to check on Cecily, and after finding she was sound asleep, I returned to my post. How late was it? I had no pocket watch, and Burtins sadly lacked a clock of any sort. I peered from a window—the bright moon had moved across the night sky. It must be very late indeed.

I yawned, stretched my limbs, and sat again. When I awoke, I was lying on my own bed, fully clothed. I did not remember coming back here—no. My last memory was of being on the cool stairs, waiting. Had someone carried me? Had Tobias done so?

Three times he'd been obliged to carry me. Three times I'd revealed a weakness. I peered over at Cecily's bed. Empty. She never woke before midmorning... I rushed from the room as fear plunged deep. How could I fail this simple task? My only task?

Chapter Ten

I flung open the door and called her name. "Cecily? Cecily!"

Tobias stumbled from his room into the hall. "What is going on?" His hair was disheveled, and an angry swipe of scratches splayed across his cheek.

"Cecily isn't in her bed. I don't know where she's gone."

We both ran down the stairs. "Check the kitchen." Was her favorite place to be of late.

Mrs. Fredrickson bent over the stove, stirring a pot. Alone. No Cecily to be seen. She turned, a question in her eyes.

"Have you seen her? My sister?"

"Not yet, I haven't. Playing hidey-seek as children are wont to do, like as not." She laughed.

We tore from the room and searched everywhere.

Tobias met me in the small foyer. "She was forever wandering off at Mayfield." He shook his head.

"I've failed you, Tobias. I'm so sorry."

"Tessa, I…"

"We need to be searching." I cut him off. I'd have to make a better apology after we found her. Had she been taken like Tobias's wee nephew? *Lord, no...please not that...*

"Get your pistol, Tessa. We need to be ready for anything."

I dashed to our room and took a minute to load the weapon properly. Tears smarted. I stepped to her bed and there lay a message hastily penciled. How had I missed it? My lack of sleep along with my careless yearnings.

I didn't want to wake you. I'm going for a walk. –C.

A walk? Why would she do such a thing alone? Unease clenched my middle. Mayhap we should have informed her a little more of the dangers rather than try to protect her overly much. It was thoughtless of me, more so since I knew she was prone to wandering at night and I had not been as watchful as I should have been. She hadn't wandered in several weeks. I'd grown lax.

I carefully carried my pistol and made my way to Tobias, who looked like he'd burst from tension.

I handed the note to him. "Here—she left this on her bed."

He snatched the paper and read. "Foolish child. But still, I cannot condone her wandering. It isn't safe until the situation with Cummins is squared away."

We exited the front doors. "I'll check the sables," Tobias shouted over his shoulder, "You walk the perimeter."

I obeyed. If she were truly lost—or taken, Tobias would never forgive me. I'm not sure I would forgive myself either.

"Cecily!" I shouted. I was so very angry with myself for not giving her my full attention. No, I had to pine and wait for

Tobias on the cold stairs last night like a love-sick debutante. I was such a fool.

The sun had fully risen. Tobias shouted her name repeatedly. Others among the small staff joined in. I made my way to the overlook where Tobias and I had hidden while waiting for Cummins to escape, but a few days ago.

I gazed down at the castle ruins. Somehow, I knew she was there, like I had an inner compass pointing to the child. Tobias ran to my side and paused.

"I think she is among the ruins." I pointed. I didn't think. I intrinsically knew.

"Why would she take a walk there in the dark? Wouldn't that be frightening for a young girl?"

"Not for her." We made our way down the hill. "I believe she was often out of doors at Mayfield, mostly at night. Her favorite place was the folly that shelters the Grecian woman holding grapes."

"The folly?" Surprise hit his voice.

"Indeed."

"The folly is a bit of a walk from the house. I had no idea she frequented that spot."

We entered the crumbling gates and shouted again.

Tobias paused and spoke in a choked, whispered voice. "There. She is there—on the steps."

Oh no. Exactly where he'd warned her to never go. I squinted against the sunlight and placed a hand over my eyes. True enough, she was slumped upon the highest stone step at the landing, the white of her muslin gown the only snatch of brightness amid the dark shadow. There was a long drop of empty air beneath her. The fall could kill her.

"We must not shout and wake her—that could prove a tragedy if she startles and—" he gulped. "I want you to go to her, Tessa. You are much lighter than I am—the stairs less likely to give way... I will be on the ground so I can catch her if she falls." He shook his head. "Be watchful of your footing."

I gulped at the climb. Twas steep. "Yes—good plan."

He cast another glance at his sister; his face had paled with fear. "Let me get into place first, then you may begin. Go cautiously."

I swallowed again as we walked swiftly to the tumbled interior walls of the castle steps. Fresh guilt surged. This is how Samuel lost his life—on the rotted stairs of Joseph's abandoned estate. A similar tragedy must not happen to another sibling. Nay, not if I could help it.

Tobias took his place among ancient stones and a tangle of vines whose growth had trailed off in the deep shadow of the rise. It was as though the sun never reached that place. He nodded. I was to begin my ascent.

I climbed the steep, narrow stairs worn smooth by time, yet now precariously wedged upon other stone that faltered with crumbling support.

Tobias was right to warn her off of them. Why had she disobeyed? Why had she not wakened me if she wanted fresh air? I should have been with her. A child's mind doesn't often think of consequences. *Posh.*

I lost my balance a little. What looked firm was not. I moved to the next step, then the next. Finally, I made it to her. I leaned my body fully over hers, so that when she wakened, she wouldn't startle and fall off the edge. "Cecily?" She breathed but didn't move. "Cecily. Wake up."

"Tessa?" Tobias shouted. "Is she alright?"

I jostled her. Once she slept, the child was terribly hard to wake. I jostled her again, and she emitted a small moan. "Wake up, dear. Tobias is worried."

Her eyes snapped open. She lifted her head and looked at her surroundings. "Where am I?"

"The castle stair. Were you having dreams about being a princess?"

"Princess..." She mumbled. "No." She peered over the edge.

"Why did you come without me?"

She shifted her weight toward the wall that ought to be secure, buried one arm around my waist. "You were sleeping. And I was ever so hot."

Last night wasn't warm, it had been cool enough I'd worn sleeves. I put my hand to her forehead. She was burning. Ill. "Don't make any sudden moves and don't let go of me. I'm going to get you down."

"I can climb down myself."

"Your brother will have my head if you do."

Her lips formed an "o". "I didn't mean to disobey." Her voice wavered. "I was so terribly hot. Now I'm freezing cold.

Indeed, the day was warming.

"We must get you to Mrs. Fredrickson, yes? Get some hot porridge into you."

"And tea. Might I have tea? I'm so cold."

I shouted down. "She is ill Tobias."

He swore.

We made our descent slowly. Each step was an accusation of my neglect. Fevers could be dangerous. Depending... One could not be too careful.

Tobias shifted position as we moved downward and finally to safety.

"Thank God." He took her up in his arms.

"I am stronger than before, Tobias. Please put me down." Her little demand bespoke the woman she'd become. He did as bid.

"I'm sorry and I will do as you tell me. I will go to bed, stay in bed, and not wander out of doors without Tessa, but first, I want you to listen."

He gave her a fatherly nod. "Indeed, you will stay in bed if I have shackle you."

She winced. Not the best words to use for a girl who had been bound to her room for far too many hours of her short life. No wonder she'd sneak to wander about Mayfield's grounds.

"As I was saying to Tessa, I got too hot, so I went outside. I saw a shadow and thought to chase it."

His brows rose. "You thought to chase a shadow?"

"He ran here. I thought him a knight wakened."

"Cecily, you know ghosts aren't real."

"I realize that now. But I was hot and it seemed so at the time." She shrugged. "I chased him here. Only it wasn't a knight at all, it was that rude man that you kicked from Burtins. The one Tessa found drunk behind the chapel altar."

Tobias gave me a look loaded with meaning. I would also be kicked from Burtins and I did not blame him. "Interesting." He asked her another question. "You followed him all the way here?"

Cecily looked confused but nodded. "I did."

"Did he see you?" I asked.

"No, but he almost did. I was afraid, so I climbed the stairs. I heard him coming. Since everyone here knows not to go up them, I didn't think they would see me. They didn't."

"Not entirely unwise given the situation—wait a minute—they? Was there more than one man?"

She nodded. "Another man joined him. They fought."

"Where?"

"You need spectacles." She pointed. "They fell asleep, too. I'm not afraid of them now that you are here."

We looked where she pointed. There were indeed two men. One Cummins, the other, unmistakably the imposter look alike. Patrick Audlington. Bile rose in my throat.

Tobias put a finger to his lips and whispered. "We must be very quiet so as to not wake them."

He played a gentle game with his sister. They were asleep, indeed. This was no lie. But they would never wake. This I could see. *Dear God...*

Tobias scooped Cecily in his arms as she whispered. "Can I go to bed now? I'm so cold." She shuddered. She was cold but a sweat had broken upon her forehead. She was truly ill.

"Tessa, I will see her to bed and situate Mrs. Fredrickson beside her. I will send Uncle to town for the doctor—and the magistrate." He nodded towards my pistol. "There is your weapon. I need you to guard the—men." He'd been about to say bodies. "Be sure no one disturbs them."

"They cannot do me harm. I will do as you ask."

He shifted Cecily to lay across his shoulder. "I hate asking." Compassion lit his eyes.

"I am capable."

"I know." His warm eyes barely grazed mine. "I'll return as soon as I can."

He left me alone with the bodies. As Tobias approached the gate, he turned back once to look at me—to be sure I hadn't abandoned my post as I had with his sister? Losh. I should have been vigilant. I took a deep breath of summer air. This eve couldn't come soon enough. I was tired, through and through. Tired of myself, my heart, my longing. The crazed events of yesterday that made me think my husband was alive.

And here he was—the man who'd stolen Patrick's name—dead. Gone. There would be no questioning him now. A true dead end.

I needed a strong cup of tea. Or a tall pot of coffee. I suddenly longed for the sea and its fresh breezes. I longed for an extended nap on the sand, in the sun where I wouldn't burn but be entirely warmed by it, inside and out. An escape from every vulnerable situation I'd found myself in. Had I not encouraged Emma with this truth? I was born to live this day. I didn't shut my eyes, but I prayed over this part of the story that I must live—whatever would come of it.

I picked up my pistol and tentatively made my way to the bodies. Mouths slacked, a trickle of blood down them—thank God their eyes were closed. It did seem like they were sleeping.

Seeing this version of Audlington brought flashes of memory back of my dear husband. Seeing him in the morgue. How alike they were! I stuffed my emotions and memories aside and drew even closer to observe him. Same facial structure, jawline, and hair. But so many little differences, he could never add up to being the man I'd once wed.

Of a sudden, I realized that there might have easily been an illegitimate child—somewhere in the family line. Patrick's father had a brother who had died while young. Could it be his offspring? Patrick's father would never—or would he? I did not know. But the likeness was uncanny.

How tragic. Even Cummin's death—brutish man—such a waste of a good living to be had. Looking at these soulless forms, I did not know what to think or say. "I give them to You, God, Creator of all things."

I wondered how they'd died together. And that's when I saw. How had I missed it? The dark places on their coats—blood. Gaping holes. They'd been shot. In this deep, dark shadow of this tower, I'd missed how the blood pooled beneath them.

They'd both been sitting when it happened. One slumped against the other. Had they been sleeping as Cecily thought?

Had they been waiting for someone? How had the gunfire not wakened her? Ah, but she was so ill with fever. She'd been delirious.

After everything she'd already been through, I hoped upon hope she did not see what had happened. Again, my failure pressed.

I glanced at the top step where she'd perched. Twas a clear view of the men. I shut my eyes against the horror. However, it was dark and she did believe them to be sleeping. Perhaps God made her stay asleep to avoid the trauma. I hoped, I willed it to be so.

I heard the sound of footsteps approaching. Was too soon for Tobias to have returned. I glanced about for a place to hide. I slipped behind a fragment of a wall, hardly enough to hide my form.

A man grunted, shifted one of the bodies. "Where is it, you scoundrel?" He muttered. "Trying to pull one over me, eh?"

My heart pounded. I recognized the voice. Had Audlington betrayed him? I slowly cocked the hammer of my pistol, wincing at the snap sound it made. I could take the man. My palms grew slick as a stab of fear pinned me in place. Tobias had all but commanded me to never to try take a man without help. I might not have a choice in the matter. Whoever this was must be the criminal. The one who had killed both of the men. He would likely be armed.

The pistol burned in my hand. How dare this person kill! How dare he further evil on Burtins' land!

A voice shouted. Tobias.

The man muttered an oath.

"Wait, stop!" Tobias shouted again.

A gun fired. The killers. At Tobias? With a shriek, I lurched from my hiding place, aimed, and shot the man in the arm—it was as I thought. The man who'd been dining with the imposter yesterday at the inn.

"Tessa!" Tobias shouted from the gates. Another man ran with a sack across his back, from the chapel. The killer ran towards him.

I looked at Tobias, he aimed and fired. Missed. The men disappeared down a steep hill just as Tobias reached me, bent over and panting. He placed a hand on my shoulder. "I must get you out of here. Burtins isn't safe. Not at all."

My hands clenched tightly around my pistol. My heart pumped too quickly and once again, I struggled to regain composure after firing.

"Tessa?" He straightened as my hands began to shake. Fire filled my veins. "Here—give me your pistol." He set his gun down and put both of his hands around mine. "You can release it now. It's going to be all right."

My arms weakened and I grew dizzy. I did not want to be weak in front of him. Failure that I was.

"Take a deep breath." The very sound of his voice soothed my spirit.

I did as told.

"Again."

I took another deep breath.

He eased the gun from my hands and slipped it into his coat pocket. "Come." He wrapped his arms around me, drawing my head to his chest. We stood like this for several minutes as I worked to overcome the aftermath.

I'd not had to actively shoot at real people since I'd been trained. The after-effects took a toll on my body and soul. Mayhap I needed to strengthen my mind. Would it help?

"You are brave enough to be sure." As he'd mentioned before. "I think you do not like to hurt people. Wicked or not."

This was true. Deep inside of me, I despised what man could do to another. How it grieved God since Cain and Able.

"Yet you will protect—regardless of what it costs you."

I drew away from him. The cost could be high if Cecily didn't get well. Voices echoed across the ruins.

"I sent the stable boy to summon some of the men from the cottages." He looked to the gates. "Here they are."

Mr. Ode led three men through the gates and towards us. One carried old blankets. To cover the bodies, no doubt.

Tobias spoke to the stable boy. "Young Tim, please escort Miss Smith back to Burtins, will you?"

Tobias whispered in my ear. "Stay with Cecily—but do stay in the room and get some rest. Send for anything you might require. I will come back to you as soon as I can."

I would not sleep until I saw her well. Not a wink.

Chapter Eleven

Mrs. Fredrickson was an absolute angel. She brought a tray with a steaming pot of tea, toast, jam, bacon, and porridge. It seemed a feast after the long night and shocking morning. She'd already bathed, fed, and tucked Cecily into bed.

"I've tended many a fever, Miss. There be a bucket of hot water should you require it. And here—" she pointed to the small brass bell on my food tray. "When ye be wanting help, stand outside your door and ring this."

She'd left a stack of handkerchiefs, towels, an empty bucket should dear Cecily become sicker, and a little vase of flowers. "Life wards away death, my dear." She smiled brightly—too brightly. A tear shimmered in her eye. If she'd tended many a fever, then she knew—we all knew what could come of them. Losh, but we were so vulnerable within this broken world!

She wagged her finger at me. "Do eat up and keep your strength. Looks as though you could do with a sleep too."

I nodded. "Thank you, Mrs. Fredrickson."

She cast a sympathetic glance at Cecily and left us.

I ate the feast before me with a thankful heart. As concerned as I was, I had to take this moment as a gift. A graceful sustenance to see me through to the next part of this challenging day.

Cecily blinked awake, her pale blonde hair splayed across her pillows. "Tessa."

I moved close to her side.

"There was thunder and lightning last night. Did it rain? I did not feel it rain. Rain would feel so good on my skin."

I put my hand on her forehead. Still burning hot. I snatched a cloth, dipped it in the cool water from the washstand, and bathed her face. The fever had deluded the truth. Mother nature had not cracked the earth with light and sound but the actions of the wicked.

Cecily took a long breath and weakly spoke. "It's raining..." The water I bathed her face with made her think it. I hoped it brought her peace and that she'd never realize what she'd actually heard. She drifted off to sleep once more. The doctor couldn't arrive quickly enough.

Two hours passed, but it seemed like no time. Not with all the thoughts swirling about my mind. Tobias didn't want us to stay here—where would we go? And would he still need me? But Cecily was ill and I knew he wouldn't dare move her. Not until she was well. That could take several days.

I looked from the window and saw Mr. Mulls returning with the magistrate in tow, the doctor nowhere to be seen.

The stable boy took the horse and led the hack away. Tobias rushed to greet the magistrate. They shook hands and Tobias led the way back to the ruins. A soft knock sounded. I opened the door and stepped out. Mr. Mulls.

"How does she fare? Poor lass."

"Her fever is still high," I said.

"Oh dear." He rubbed a hand over his whiskered chin. "The doctor was seeing another patient and will be delayed. He will be another hour arriving, at least. He sends his regrets that he could not come sooner."

"Thank you for relaying the message."

He continued. "I am sickened, Miss Smith. Sickened that so much has been happening on these grounds. That it has become…" He shrugged with his hands out. "Used to be a peaceful place until…"

"Until what, Mr. Mulls?"

"Until it came into Chinworth hands." He shook his head. "I hate saying it. My sister-in-law's family weren't the best people but at least I could live in peace here. Not that I blame Tobias, mind you, but…to think that death has come upon this place! Unthinkable. Not to mention, I was nearly killed." He turned to go. "Someone wanted me dead. Wanted someone in London to think me dead and buried." He pressed a hand to his heart. "I am a threat to none. I am neither involved nor am I privy to any intrigues. Aside from Cummins's gambling and whatnot. I can't imagine that my life matters a whit to anyone."

"That cannot be true."

He shrugged. "The children do enjoy their kites."

"A happy childhood is important. If a child can achieve many happy days—maybe as the result of a well-made kite, you will have done the child a service. Children don't forget the happy days and what constituted them. When they are older, they will reach into the past and the memory will give them hope when times are hard." I put a hand on his arm. "You aren't just making kites; you offer the heights of hope."

A smile lit his face. "Amid the grim reality, my dear, *you* have given me hope. I will pray for the child. She must live to fly her kite."

"Indeed. She must live to do a great many things."

He bowed.

"Thank you, Mr. Mulls."

The kind gentleman seemed a bully at first, but he did much to put me at ease. He was a caring soul. The only true gruffness about him was the shaggy gray head of hair.

I retrieved a pencil and foolscap and sat again beside Cecily. I thought about the events surrounding my husband's death. Why anyone possibly related to him would take on his name? It seemed a dangerous venture to do so, especially since I've had to use a different name so as not to be discovered.

Patrick, the real Patrick, had gone to the shipyard that morning to collect a payment on behalf of his employer. He must have seen or heard something not meant for his ears. Something utterly condemning. His employer had been demanding an overdue payment. Perhaps they did not have the funds. But why kill the messenger? No, it had to be something Patrick found out. He had to be eliminated. They'd come after me and Joseph in case—in case he'd told us about it?

There hadn't been time to do so. He was dead. Unless...unless Patrick knew sooner—discovered information sooner than the day of his death.

I squeezed my eyes shut and tried to remember the days before the tragedy. Those blissfully happy weeks I'd blocked out of my mind to survive the grief. How ignorant I'd been about the future I'd have to survive. The days leading up had been good. Patrick was lighthearted, more than usual. We were planning a trip to Scotland.

I stood and paced, reaching into the distant memory. We were going to be gone for an extended time...

"But what about your work?" I queried. I was tired of combating societal gossip.

He grinned. "My work can wait, and you know I can afford to do as I wish."

I did indeed. My husband had chosen work instead of being an idle gentleman.

"Buy fresh gowns, darling. And anything you might require."

"Anything?" I laughed as I wiped jam from his chin with my napkin.

"We leave in three days."

"Three days? Not near enough time to buy cloth and have gowns made, you know. I can't possibly be ready."

He lifted me off my feet and spun me around. "Order the trunks brought down. Fill them as you will." He kissed me and left for work.

I'd never see him alive again.

The joy of those plans blackened into sorrow as I'd never known. Patrick hadn't come home for supper. Joseph offered to fetch him from his office. When he found it empty, his employer had been equally confused about his absence. He gave Joseph directions to his last known location. He wasn't there, but by pure coincidence—or by God's hand—Joseph had taken a shortcut under the docks. There he'd found Patrick's body.

After getting the attention of the constabulary, his body had been hauled away. Joseph made his way to me to break the news. Only he'd been followed. We were attacked.

I paced the bedroom floor as the memories flooded. And paced some more. Patrick knew something before his death. The sudden plans to travel to Scotland had been out of the blue. He wanted to get away. He knew something, but what? Joseph and I had turned it round and around and we could never find an answer.

Whatever secret Patrick held had died with him. But why resurrect his name? Who was that man trying to fool?

Definitely his killer—the one I'd shot as he ran off.

Mrs. Fredrickson opened the door, an anxious look over her brow. "Pardon me, Miss Smith, but Mr. Chinworth asked me to bring you this message." She handed me a scrap of paper.

I opened and read.

Tessa,

The Audlington imposter clings to life, but near death's door. Bringing him inside. Wanted you to know, but not to fear.

—Tobias

He was alive. I sank into the chair by Cecily's bed.

Mrs. Fredrickson approached. "I hope you aren't ill too?"

"Not at all. Do you have time to brew a pot of coffee?"

She nodded. "I'll do so straight away." She left me to my wonderings. Someone wanted it believed that Mr. Mulls was dead, though he was not—was it the same someone who desired it believed that Patrick Audlington *lived*?

To what end? Nothing made sense. I needed to see the list again. Was Mr. Mulls' name on it? With a black dot by his name? We'd been too distracted by Patrick's name being listed, perhaps we didn't notice.

I needed to speak with Tobias and soon.

Chapter Twelve

A watched pot never boils. I waited for Tobias for what seemed like an eternity. The young doctor had come and gone. Evidently, the fever had been flying about the village and was expected to lift within a few days. I hoped that would be the case for Cecily. The trip to the village had been hard on her vulnerable body. She needed more fruit and vegetables, he said. More red meat. Less porridge.

She had a fondness for porridge. I would try to build her appetite for better things. I was so relieved to learn that children weren't dying of this sickness.

By the time Tobias arrived, Cecily was sitting up in bed, picking at a bowl of boiled potatoes and cabbage, swimming in chicken broth.

I was anxious to tell him my thoughts but couldn't speak in front of Cecily. He seemed to be anxious as well. He'd tossed his jacket aside in the summer heat; his cravat had been loosened. He approached his sister. "The doctor says not to worry. You'll be right as rain in a few days."

Cecily lifted her small chin. "Then I can't go back to baking with Mrs. Fredrickson?"

He smiled. "Indeed you may." His brows lifted. "Tessa. A word?" He gestured to the hall. We exited the room and he shut the door behind him.

First things first. "Tobias. I am so very sorry. I understand if you feel the need to replace me with someone more competent."

Shock registered on his face. "Why would I replace you?"

"Because I fell asleep and—I did not see to Cecily when she needed me. I—do you not wish to replace me?"

His lips parted in clear surprise. "No. Exhaustion is not a crime. My sister is a special case. While we must be vigilant, she must also make the right choices."

"It could have ended badly."

"Agreed. But it did not."

"No…" It hadn't. In fact, if she hadn't wandered to the ruins, we wouldn't have discovered the bodies, or come face to face with the killer.

"Does she remember much more?"

"She does not. I suppose you saw that the men had been shot?"

"Yes."

"Cecily thought it thunder and lightning in her fevered state. I don't believe she was able to see what really happened."

"Thank God."

"Yes."

"The imposter still lives?"

"He does. The doctor is tending him now. The magistrate is with him."

"Did you search the crawl spaces last night? With Mr. Ode?"

"We did. Tis an adventure I'd rather not enjoy again. But all we found was an empty cellar with footprints that might have been there for ages for all I know." He shrugged. "Was built in an unusual space—the only entry we could find is through the wine cellar. If there is an exit, I don't know of it. Cummins knew his way around Burtins. I wonder his other secrets? He is beyond explaining any of them now."

"It is tragic. But Tobias—if there was only one way in or out—"

His lips quirked. "He somehow made it out before I ventured within."

I cringed. The way to the cellar was dark and steep. Positioned in a small corner off the scullery where the game hung, fowl and rabbit, waiting to be cooked. Not a pleasant place, to be sure. "There is a door off the scullery."

"Just so. Convenient for the fellow. Only his escape ended a deadly one."

"Has Audlington awoken?"

"He is yet unconscious. He might not recover." He grimaced. "I'm sorry to put you through this." He shifted on his feet. "You are certain, Tessa, that he isn't your—"

"He is not. I am completely certain." I caught warmth in his eyes. "Perchance a relative, but no. I am sure it isn't him."

"It's an odd twist to our true to life tale." He took one of his deep breaths and exhaled slowly.

"I'm sorry you have to live out this true tale, Tobias."

He folded his arms. "I shall sort it, I promise you."

But what if he couldn't? What if neither of us could go any farther with this tangle than we'd already gone? What then? Could we be content with not knowing? An unsolved mystery to add intrigue to the remainder of our days? I had to speak. I'd already gone six years with unanswered questions. One could come to peace with life as it came.

"Even if you do not, I trust that you still have a good life ahead of you."

His response drove a truth home. "If I don't, more lives may be lost. And not just mine. My nephew's... or yours? I can't let that happen. I won't let it happen."

I'd been so wrapped up in my own interior dramatics concerning my dead husband's look-alike and my guilt that I completely forgot about the wee son who would inherit Mayfield one day. Should he be found. *Lord, there is much to pray over. Help us.* I believed He would. Our Creator could see straight to the marrow of our situation. I believed He would show us the truth in time. Oft times He would only show us one step at a time, other times more. We had to trust Him no matter how hard the situation became.

Tobias's hand came under my chin. "So you see, I cannot do without you." His voice gentled. "Not for a moment."

The impact of his words slammed into my heart where it shouldn't go—but then his lips met mine. His hand gently came to the small of my back and he kissed me as though he loved me. Did he? An arm went about my waist as he pulled me closer, deepening his affection. His lips ventured to my cheek and he whispered. "I cannot do without you. I'll never deserve you, Tessa." His lips found mine again. "But I will try." He drew away. "You have my heart. I will endeavor to have yours."

Endeavor to have mine? He had it. Did he not know? He must. He reached across the small gap between us and wove his fingers into mine. My heart pounded and I couldn't speak for the beauty, the warmth of the moment. This was everything my heart had been longing for.

And then, too much happened all at once.

The magistrate shouted. A messenger arrived. A scream rent the air, and the imposter breathed a tale that sent us spinning and Tobias on a journey that quite left Cecily and I alone. Alone with the burning reminder of a kiss and a promise that he would return.

Little did I know that I would not see him again for three long months. Would that time stopped at the moment our affections flamed to life that I might tell him the full truth of my heart. I could not do so in a letter. Could I? Could I spill the contents of my heart there? If another pair of eyes read my words, would our love become endangered?

Ah. Mayhap this is why he did not expound upon much other than his general welfare in his missives.

I leaned my forehead against the window while the late summer rain dashed against it. Cecily was well. Quite well. And I? Lovesick. Quite. I blinked against the rain as though tears. I missed Tobias Chinworth. Desperately.

I thought back to our tender moment together in the hall and the events that interrupted our heart's admissions. A letter had arrived from Lord Sherborne via two of Joseph's trained men whom I recognized. They remained at Burtins, patrolling the grounds night and day regardless that we believed the miscreants who had utilized Burtins property for evil have fled.

Tobias read the letter Sherborne had sent. "When you told me your husband's name, I recognized it. From where, I did not know. Father had been sending me on all manner of errands for years. But not six years—perhaps four at the most. No longer than that. So there was not much of a chance that I'd met him. I simply couldn't recall where I'd heard his name. I queried Lord Sherborne to look at the evidence and many affidavits concerning the Banbury case to see if Patrick Audlington's name resurfaced. It has." He held up Sherborne's long missive. "A one Patrick Audlington that had been involved in some shipments. He was on the list of men who had authority to accept deliveries." Tobias pursed his lips. "These weren't just any shipments. They were Banbury's cache of weapons."

"My Patrick would never—"

"No. Not your Patrick. But this other fellow, whom the good doctor says has awoken. I must go to him."

"Have you looked again at the list of names we found on Cummins?"

"I do recall this Audlington's name being there—and how that startled you. To think we should see the man in the village soon after. It was Providential. I hope."

"Yes, but listen. Mr. Mulls was ruminating on the thought that someone should want him dead—or at the very least—that someone should think him dead. That perhaps that was the point. Someone needed to think Mulls was no longer here—at Burtins."

Tobias felt within his interior coat pocket. "I have it here." He unfolded the paper. "I've not had a moment to look at it again since yesterday morning." He scanned the names and I attempted to look over his arm. "It's there. At the bottom. See? My name, too, is next to his."

My blood ran cold.

"Failed attempts, both of them." He touched my cheek and I warmed. "One failed because of you." He read over the list again. "Cummins is not listed."

"I wonder if he is the one who wrote it."

"Perhaps. But I don't think so. I think he is working for someone else. Cummins wasn't intelligent enough run a clandestine operation."

"The other list. The weapons. Do you think they are Audlington's? The one that worked for Banbury?"

His brows rose. "Whose else could it be?"

"Tobias. Why would any of this have anything to do with Burtins?"

Tobias grimaced. "Because my dear Father hadn't relinquished his ties with Banbury as he told us. He lied. Again."

"Do you think the weapons are or," I shrugged, "were hidden here?"

"On Burtins's grounds? I have no doubt. It pains me to say it but I believe my beloved housekeeper knows more than she lets on. Do keep an eye on her, when you aren't busy with Cecily. I hate casting suspicion on the good woman but I cannot rule it out. It is possible she has been threatened to silence. Our arrival was quite unannounced and I wonder that she did not write to me concerning Uncle Mull's injury and the theft."

I hated to think it of her but there was a strong case that he was right. She, at the very least, knew something and wasn't telling. Mayhap for her own safety. Or maybe the answer was far simpler than that...

"Father practically begged me to travel here to get away from the dangerous threats. I wonder what he really intended for my arrival." He refolded the lists and placed them back into his interior coat pocket. "I will leave you to my sister. I would speak with Audlington while he lives." Intensity creased his brows.

"Might I go with you?" I was curious about the man. He had to be a relation of some sort.

"You may, but I implore you not to tell him who you are—or were, rather." He called the young maid in training to come sit with Cecily. "He lifted my hand to his lips and grazed my knuckles. "I am so relieved that man isn't your husband."

I'd been stunned by his kiss, but this pronouncement and the look in his eyes left my heart pounding. He kept my hand and led me to the sick chamber on the first floor.

The young doctor sat nearby, smoking a pipe, and the magistrate stood with folded arms. The man was propped up on several pillows, his face bruised purple and yellow. The color had deepened since I observed him at the ruins. The bandages across his stomach seeped bright red. Not a good sign.

The doctor took a puff and spoke. "He doesn't have long, poor soul. He's lost too much blood."

Tobias approached the bedside. "Shall I call for the vicar?"

A rusted voice scraped through his throat. "No time. You'll have to be vicar enough for me, if you want the job."

Dear God... It was one thing to find the men and think them already gone. Was quite another to see a man slip from this life to the next to meet his Maker, I hoped.

"But first I have to tell you—"

"No." Tobias cut him off. "You are dying, we must pray."

"But—"

"Your soul, man. Give it care in your final hour."

"Yes."

Tobias bowed and prayed. I'd not heard him do such before now. We'd only talked about praying, how the vicar at Butterton had guided him into a firm knowledge about God. And that Joseph had forgiven him. Words flowed from him. Gentle words spoken over this man's heart and soul, to be forgiven no matter how he'd lived or what he'd done.

The magistrate shifted on his feet and looked away. The doctor seemed a bit stunned. I wondered then, had they only seen men of the cloth pray? Such seemed all too common. The action made me love Tobias all the more. They didn't understand why he'd waste time praying instead of gaining information, but I knew. I understood.

I realized that Tobias's brother Zachary had no time for soul searching before his death. The wretch had joined the chase to capture Emmaline, and paid for it with his life. So had Samuel. Life had become precious to Tobias, and in the swift choice to put a man's soul above everything else, the room became a holy place.

When Tobias finished praying, a tear slipped from Audlington's eye. Then Tobias began his questioning. "What is your real name?"

"Patrick Audlington." He gave a bitter laugh. "Patrick Audlington Straight. My grandfather thought it a good punishment. Forced my mother to name me after my legitimate sibling—so that the whole village might guess from whence I came and shame her all at once."

The answer I'd suspected, but more. The poor woman...

"We look enough alike, so I'm told."

"You never met the real Patrick Audlington?"

"Never. Spied him from a distance when I was a lad, but no."

"Why did you drop your surname? Mr. Straight is a far cry from Audlington."

"You can already guess." He gasped in pain; his breath came shorter. "I was being used."

"But Mr. Audlington is known to be dead."

His hand raised a little. "Not entirely known. He wasn't popular or well-known among the ton."

This was true. He wasn't.

"This was to my benefit..."

"How so?"

"Being an illegitimate son, no matter how good you are, no matter one's high marks at school, fine manners—dress…" he coughed. "Gets doors slammed in my face. The other man's death was rather hushed, was it not?"

Had it been? I paused and returned to that time. The dark, cold day of his burial. The few people that attended. After the assailants followed Joseph and, I shut my eyes, beat us, we had to be vigilant. We'd hidden ourselves. I'd not gone to tea—I was supposed to be in Scotland, so I allowed my acquaintances to believe that's where I'd gone. The funeral was the only public appearance I'd made after the murder, however unusual it was for a woman to do so. The churchyard had been devoid of anyone, not even his employer.

He was right. It had been hushed.

He continued. "I worked in his stead."

"Who hired you?"

"That would be telling."

"You are about to die, why would it matter?"

Patrick's forehead wrinkled with pain. "Because there are things at play that you do not want to get involved in—nor your fine lady who lurks in that shadow. Let me guess, Audlington's widow?"

Tobias didn't answer him.

"What kinds of things are at play?"

"You've heard of Banbury?"

The magistrate approached. "Who hasn't?"

"The man thought he was invincible. A god." A breathy laugh escaped from his throat. "A few men desire to take his place."

The magistrate's jaw grew firm. "What kind of operation were you involved in?"

"I was merely continuing my dear dead half-brother's work."

I stalled at that. He managed finances for a large shipping company.

Tobias shot me a glance before asking another question. I would remain silent. "You keep us in suspense on purpose. You are about to die, what do you have to lose?"

The man grunted. "What if I live? Then I may still be of some use. Ol' Prinny won't like that I've told."

"I think you lie, sir."

"No, tis true. Patrick Audlington worked for the Crown until he wanted out—and died before he could resettle elsewhere." He snorted. "You'd think the Crown oblivious to the gentries' illegitimate offspring, but no. They are very aware of our existence and us our desire for a true place in the country." He coughed again. "They offer us duty and honor—and gain."

"You thought to gain."

"No. Gain is nothing to me, honor, yes. My grandfather may have burdened my shoulders with my mother's disgrace but the Crown offered me his legitimate position—and name."

I wanted to weep for this man. He'd wanted to truly own the name he'd been shouldered with. I longed for the day when little ones would not be saddled with their parent's sins and indiscretions. Did not God create all life?

"So I became Patrick Audlington. Was easy to do since we are near twins, though I but six months younger."

My mind was dizzy with too many emotions. That my father-in-law had betrayed his wife. This man had endured much of the sad consequences. And of pertinent import: my husband had really worked for the Crown? It seemed impossible. And yet...pieces began to fit. There had been many times I'd asked details of his daily work that he did not, or would not expound upon. The sudden trip to Scotland? The man made it sound as if we were resettling. No mere trip.

The magistrate grimaced. "A likely tale."

"My tale is verifiable."

"Who should I write to or visit for such verifications? Tell me that?"

Tobias held a hand out. "I believe him, but we will definitely verify his story. In due time." Tobias asked one last question. "And what brings a man of the Crown to Burtins? And," he pulled one of the lists from his pocket. "Why is your name here—with these others?" He held it in front of his face.

The man smiled. "Your name is on it, too; I might ask you the same question." His words drained from him as pain lanced his brow. He reached weakly for the list. "Everyone on this list is dead—except you. And Mr. Mulls." He licked his lips. "They will try for you again. These men are ruthless. They get what they want. The Crown gave me a legitimate name, true, but I am...expendable." He coughed. "I always was."

Tobias knotted his fists. "Why do they want me dead?"

"A Chinworth has more than one enemy. Take note. The people that had me shot? You are merely in the way. This list..." he shook his head. "Is rather telling. Now I know who double-crossed me." He took a deep breath and shuddered. The doctor rushed to his side.

"The pain is..." His eyes closed, "Bad."

The doctor spoke. "He suffers greatly."

I made my way to the side of his bed. "Is there anything you can do for him?"

The man nodded. "I have done so already. Time will tell."

Tobias nudged Patrick's shoulder. "Who double-crossed you?"

The man's lips moved.

"Can you speak louder?" Tobias urged.

"Would be treason for me to say it." He moaned but kept talking. "Burtins was being used to hide a cache of weaponry for a manipulated uprising here, on English soil. The weaponry has been moved." He clenched his teeth. "To Mayfield Manor, I believe."

No. How awful!

Tobias gave me a meaning-filled glance. His father had possibly arranged to scare Tobias away—he was still pulling strings like a puppeteer. Who else could have done this?

"Can't imagine a small village like Butterton the location of an uprising."

"The cache was to travel from there to London, where my cohorts would take it. Only..."

Only?

He struggled for breath. "Mercy, God. Have mercy on me."

In a rash moment, I grabbed the man's hand. I wished someone had been there to do so for my husband in his final moments. He'd been alone. So very alone.

Then, with a final shudder of breath, he was gone.

He'd worked for Banbury—and the Crown...He spoke of treason...had the Crown manipulated him? He called himself expendable. May it never be said of anyone. The hushed moments after his death were pregnant with information that still needed sorting.

Then Tobias left with all haste to follow the cache to Mayfield—to speak with his Father— and I did not know what else.

Aside from the guards Joseph sent, I'd been left completely alone, a part of my heart gone with him.

Chapter Thirteen

Cecily and I received a letter from Tobias nearly every week, though its contents were sometimes two weeks behind. It irked me not knowing the details of his doings, whether or not they found the cache, and whether he was safe. Did he have a lead on where his infant nephew resided?

Here at Burtins, our guardians were ever vigilant, even ensuring my kit was properly stocked with supplies to fill my pistol. They encouraged me to practice with them a few times a week while Cecily baked in the kitchen with Mrs. Fredrickson. I could see that the men were bored. No intrigues or enemies remained at Burtins since Cummins and Mr. Straight died. So I hoped. There was little action aside from the mail post arriving. I clung to Tobias's words

My dearest Tessa,

I remember our discussion in the hall before I left. The way you responded. Note that I will endeavor to do what I stated. I promise you...

He spoke of our embrace. His kiss. His promise to be worthy of me...and again he wrote:

My dearest Tessa,

Whatever gave you the thought that you should leave? I hope you never think I would desire your absence ever again, no matter what happens. I never want you to leave my side...but should you choose to do so...

It would never be so. When would I be brave enough to tell him? His words were always few, but full of the few times we'd all but declared our hearts. My heart would burst before he returned.

We were left to the peaceful quiet of this countryside. Cecily improved by leaps and bounds. She began to behave like a young woman and not the wild child I'd first met some months ago. We'd even successfully weaned her from the terrible elixir. I hoped she would never be trapped by such a drug again.

I was glad the difficulties were out of reach. Cecily needed this kind of peace and quiet. Mr. Mulls became a thorough Uncle, who made her not one but several kites to fly over the unused fields.

The months had passed, and my stack of letters had grown, except of late. Deliveries ended, I could not guess why. Autumn pressed in. How much longer would we be left to heal and languish at Burtins? Might Tobias spare me some information? If not by mail, at least a short visit? Indeed, there had been no letter last week or this. Mrs. Fredrickson called the mail service unpredictable. But I was beginning to worry and my patience wore thin.

Kite weather turned into mid-October's colorful trees and fierce autumnal gales, and Cecily and I read many a book by a warm fire. Life was too calm, and the peace I'd felt over the warmer months began to fade into the realization that something was simmering beneath. My spirit stirred. Something was afoot, and something was very wrong. I sensed a new tension in the air, though I did not know why.

The maid that Mrs. Fredrickson had trained whistled the same familiar tune as she scrubbed the upper hall floor. Mr. Ode was gentle enough. While he preferred to work in the fields, he understood the gravity of Tobias's situation. He gladly took up the position of steward temporarily. I believed I could trust him.

The tenants had accepted the change—as several of the men reported to Tobias when we'd first arrived, they were wary of the dangers that Cummins had brought to their lives. As it were, since Cummins's departure from this life, the gatherings and gambling had ceased. Their young daughters were safe from the many gentlemen who would ravish them given the chance. I'd half a mind to train the girls to defend themselves as I had been. But my first duty was to Cecily. Like as not, the fathers wouldn't allow it. Pride would get in the way as they desired to be their daughter's first and only defender until marriage. One day perhaps fathers would see that they were protecting them by allowing the training.

I squinted against the faint sun peeking through deep gray clouds. A chill scampered across my spine. There was something off about the air beyond the natural decay. I began to fear.

I prayed that God would send Tobias back to us or send for us at the very least. Answers were needed. Tobias was needed.

I'd observed Mrs. Fredrickson as he requested and if she knew anything at all, she kept it well-tucked within. Maybe she didn't know much beyond the woman's work at Burtins. Her affection for Cecily increased. The granddaughter she never had, she'd told me. But the woman had grown quieter of late. I wondered if she felt the same sense of unease that I did.

I was not to wonder long.

I finally received a hastily written message from Tobias.

My love, do what she says. You can trust her. Stay with Cecily. Ever yours, Tobias.

Who was she?

I found out in the middle of the night.

Mrs. Fredrickson.

"Come lasses, and come quick. They are upon us and must not find you here. I beg you to wake up and gather a few belongings."

"What is the meaning of this?" I asked her, my hand crept towards my pistol laying ready. Of late, I'd taken to remaining dressed. The unease had put me on edge. I felt I needed to be ready for anything.

She too, was dressed in a cloak with a bundle as though she did not intend to stay. "I mean you no harm, but *they* arrive this night—men who mustn't be here, devil take them. We have little time."

"How do you know this?"

"Mr. Chinworth."

"Older or younger?" I'd not forgotten Tobias's request that I observe her. I'd found nothing to be concerned about, only kindness.

"Master Tobias, of course. None else do I trust. Come, gather the child. I'll not see you being harmed for anything."

"Where do we go? Should we not take Mr. Mulls with us?"

"Believe me, I tried. Mulls won't be persuaded. He'll stay where they'll expect him to be. If he leaves they will wonder at his departure. No, I'm to see my elderly sick mother and Mr. Mulls will keep an eye on things." She must have seen the concern on my face. She took my hand and squeezed it. "The young master provided him with a pistol. He will defend himself if need be."

"What about the guards?"

She grinned a wide, toothy smile. "They await you under the portico. Horses are saddled." Her eyes shimmered with a tear. "You must trust me young lass. The note from Master Tobias is true." She stuffed a few of Cecily's things into a sack. "The guards have been warned. They'll not leave yours and Cecily's side."

"Where are we to go?"

"Not far, but far enough."

"Our guardians know?"

Again, she smiled. "Tobias told me to look out for you both. I'm doing the best I can. But you need to hurry. You carry the child, I'll get your bags."

I had to toss my doubts aside. I didn't really know if I could trust Mrs. Fredrickson this far. I hoped I could but in this vulnerable moment? I shoved a stack of clean handkerchiefs into my reticule, trying to think clearly. Regardless of the situation, I could trust the men Joseph had sent to help. Seemed I had no other choice. Tobias would want me to leave—isn't that what he'd meant by the hasty message? To "do what she says?" He'd not specified who, and that concerned. Why hadn't he been more direct?

A question plunged a very real possibility. Had I not received letters because they'd been stolen? He had to be careful not to mention names. Indeed, he was careful in all of his messages as was I, aside from the few affectionate remarks. He was in danger and we would be too if we did not leave with all haste.

Fear surged as we made our way down the stairs and to the waiting men. They were alert, glancing about the grounds, jaws tight. The one named Thomas offered a nod. "Miss Smith, we are at your service. We must require cooperation from you and the girl if we are to adequately protect you."

"I understand." Did they, too, sense what I had over the past days? Had they received a message too? I wanted to ask, to sort out what little information we had between us. Especially of Mrs. Fredrickson. She gave us each a kiss on the cheek and patted mine with her gloved hand. "Tell Master Tobias that I will return when…" She swallowed at her own emotion. "When he cleans house."

I knew what she meant. "Thank you. For everything."

She spoke to the guards. "Go before it's too late."

Unfortunately, we had to share riding the horses. Cecily grumbled at being woken, but I told her we must and she did not argue. Her trust in me was unwavering. I hoped not futile.

The wind whistled among the trees surrounding the grounds. The guard's jaws were set with purpose. We climbed into our saddles. The one named Thomas pulled me behind him and off we went, along the sides of the main road, nearest the trees and hedges. I prayed unceasingly as we went, being as vigilant as Joseph had taught me.

If we were in true danger, I must be ready to help Cecily—with my life, if need be.

The few hours of travel were mercifully uneventful. Just before dawn, the guards pulled the horses close together and consulted on directions that I had more than once wished they would share with me. A few minutes later, we rode down a long private lane shadowed by arches of great maple trees.

Soon, I stood in a grand foyer and next, in Tobias Chinworth's arms.

Chapter Fourteen

I breathed in his scent, relished the feel of his warmth encircling me, and wept. Cecily had squealed with glee and embraced him before being led away by a young maid for breakfast and a rest, leaving us alone. I peered after her, reluctant to be separated from my charge.

Tobias reassured me. "She is quite alright. We are safe here. I promise."

After being her guardian night and day, it was hard to let her leave my sight. Especially after the night she'd wandered to the ruins while I slept. But that was months ago, and now... Tears threatened again as I gazed upon him.

Tobias stroked my cheek with the side of his thumb. When I looked into his eyes, they too, were shining with tears. Had he been afraid?

He spoke my name in a whisper as though he'd longed for me as I did him. "Tessa." He leaned his head against mine. "I hoped you would come. I feared you might not trust my message—I realized my mistake. I'd written it too quickly. I should have been more direct—more informative. I wasn't clear enough."

What mattered was that we were together again. My heart was near to bursting. "I did wonder if I was doing the right thing. But I somehow knew I was supposed to leave Burtins as Mrs. Fredrickson said. Regardless, Joseph's men were our protectors. I knew I could trust them at the very least."

"A cache was being moved to Burtins overnight. Though Banbury is dead, some of the workings of his operations continue under the Crown's nose—and some within plain sight. Whatever suits the Crown is allowed by the Crown." He smirked. "Unwise as it may be."

"They cannot continue to utilize your property..."

"No, indeed not. The militia will be upon them to seize it and arrest the men involved." He smiled. "We are out of danger, Tessa."

"We are?" I loved the way he said my name.

He nodded with a gentle smile. "I feel like I can truly breathe for the first time in a long time."

"Where are we?"

"Westhill Park, about fifteen miles south of Burtins."

"Oh?"

"Lord Oberton is a good friend of Sherborne's. I'd not been introduced to him until last night—he is a good sort. The old gent helped Sherborne take Banbury down. One of the few men Banbury hadn't managed to manipulate."

He drew me across an opulent foyer of lavish floral arrangements and gilded mirrors—I caught a glimpse of myself. Disheveled, hair falling. I was undeniably rumpled. Tobias didn't seem to care, so I could not. Had we not seen each other at our best and worst? He led me into a quiet drawing room. Pale blues and creams lent a calming air, the red Turkish rug a generous dash of warmth. Twas altogether pleasant. Tea was brought, the maid quietly set the tray on tea table and left us alone.

We sat upon the settee, he wove his fingers mine. I had so many questions, I wasn't sure where to start. "What of your father? What did he tell you?"

Tobias took a deep breath, shaking his head. "My father...admitted to nothing. When I plied him, I didn't tell him that Cummins was dead—or about Mr. Straight. But he knew. Somehow, he knew."

"Someone at Burtins told him?"

"Or someone in the village is involved. I imagine more than a few men are. According to Mr. Ode, not just strangers frequented Cummins's parties. Villagers too. The operation wouldn't work without them. Not only that, but someone in Butterton." He closed his eyes and shook his head. "There is no end to this tangle."

"Do you think the magistrate knows?"

"He does by now. I visited my father a few times but all he wanted to know was if Cecily was well. At least he cares about her."

"You think he doesn't care about you?"

"I don't know." Tobias shrugged. "His way of showing regard isn't always in the most nurturing manner."

I thought of the dangerous elixir he'd tried to use to fix his daughter—the same elixir that he'd slipped to Emma and put her to sleep so she wouldn't leave Mayfield—and mayhap killed her grandfather. We would never know the true ramifications of the drug. There was no singular cure-all for every illness or ill temper. Even so, I pitied the man. While he'd covered his sins with lies and manipulations, he'd also lost so much.

"When Father begged me to leave Mayfield and go to Burtins, I didn't know what to think. But after the attempt on my life and the threatening message, I took his advice. I did need to go to Burtins and begin reorganizing the estate. I believed he wanted me away from danger, but in truth, he wanted me away from Mayfield as the cache was being transferred from Burtins to Butterton."

Of course. Did the man not realize his life was on the line? Why did he still play at these games? "Had it been moved?"

"Indeed, but I was too late."

"How did you know?"

"Sherborne had men watching and we found evidence. With so few staff remaining at Mayfield, it was easy for them to hide it."

"What did you hope to do if you caught them?" Tobias had no army at his command.

"I don't know. It had already been taken to London from there. Lord Sherborne and I followed, but the weapons had been too well hidden. We took the opportunity to check on Mr. Straight's story—posing as Patrick Audlington."

My stomach did a little flip. I'd been oblivious about the life my husband had been leading, and the man that became his replacement. "And?"

He grimaced. "Was a drastic mistake on our part. Thanks to Lord Sherborne's connections, we were released, but not without a promise, which was easy to give. An exchange of information concerning what we'd discovered about Banbury's caches of weapons. Thus, why we had to act quickly last night. We traveled night and day to get here—and rescue you and Cecily from potential danger."

"You were gone so long—the whole of summer."

"The Crown detained us. Lady Sherborne was none too pleased—I will have to make it up to them somehow." He laughed. "They released Lord Sherborne after a few weeks, but because I, being a Chinworth whose father awaits trial, was a suspect."

"No! But—."

He squeezed my hand. "I can't say I blame them. Father's deeds reached deeper than I knew." His voice trailed as I poured a cup of tea and handed it to him. He sipped. "I make the same decision in their shoes."

"Why didn't you tell me?" I would have prayed over it specifically—and done something, anything to help.

His voice gentled. "Can you not guess why I did not tell you?"

I could only think of how I would have stopped at nothing to see him free. I loved him. I would conceal the fact no longer.

"You are Patrick Audlington's widow. They assume you know nothing—that you are living somewhere in Scotland as Audlington had originally planned for you." He smiled. "They grossly underestimated you and what you've been doing since."

Indeed. I'd trained to defend myself and worked to defend another, if the need arose. I poured myself a cup of the strong brew and added cream. I was never one to simply sit by and wait for life to happen.

Tobias continued. "If you'd revealed yourself, they would have suspected that you were involved. They would have detained you, too—and for what? And for how long? I couldn't let that happen to you. Cecily needed you. You aren't involved. Not in that way."

I drank my tea, hot and soothing, very aware that Tobias hadn't taken his eyes from me. His regard warmed more than the tea. My heart thrummed as the strength of my feelings matched his. I wanted to weep and laugh at the same time.

"Don't you see? I needed you safe. I had to protect you." He took the cup from my hands and settled it within the saucer. "I need you, Tessa." His hand came beneath my jaw as his lips met mine. How I dreamed what it would be like to be kissed once again by the man who had my heart and wouldn't let go! He was so soft and gentle that I did begin to weep at the joy of being near him again. I couldn't help it.

No, indeed. I would never again have to conceal my affection.

He kissed me until the tea grew quite cold but our hearts were afire. He drew back only when the butler entered and inquired to know if we still needed breakfast. The interruption, a sudden event that had us laughing. The look on the poor butler's face.

Tobias led me into the dining room where a morning's feast awaited—and Lord Oberton. The man approached as Tobias introduced us. "Miss Smith, Lord Oberton has been anxious to make your acquaintance."

The gentleman, though short in stature, was entirely handsome. I'd seen him before, at Almacks—years ago. His dark blonde hair with silvered sides bespoke his age, near forty I suspected, and single. More than one mother plotted on behalf of their daughters during the Season.

The man amicably grinned. "Let us away with façade, Chinworth. I know Audlington's widow when I see her." He remembered me as I did him. I flinched as He took my hand as he bowed. Was he truly safe?

He must have sensed my reticence. "Do not be concerned, my lady. It is my intent that you are seen and known for who you are and what you have endured. Nothing else. You have my greatest respect." He turned to Tobias and bowed. "As this man is fast gaining my esteem. Never thought I'd be able to trust a Chinworth."

Tobias laughed. "Nor did I think to trust a stranger such as yourself."

He laughed. "Without Sherborne, we'd be lost, eh? Come, seat yourselves and Sunning will serve us." The Butler saw to my plate first, then Tobias's. Then Lord Oberton's. Both tea and coffee were brought, with plenty of cream. After the long night of riding, the full breakfast was heavenly.

Lord Oberton spoke. "Young Miss Chinworth has been settled within her chamber and my best maid is regaling her with stories. I believe they've become fast friends."

I'd wondered how she fared. She did not like to part with me for long. I would check on her as soon as I'd finished breakfast. But I had to inquire. "How did you know me to be Audlington's widow?" While he was easily recognizable, his status was far above mine.

"I remembered you." He smiled. "Not to sound puffed but I don't forget a face. Never have."

"An admirable ability, to be sure."

He laughed. "Sherborne told me, not that I needed him to do so. He knows we cannot have secrets between us, even of the smallest consequence. There have oft been mistakes made on the hinge of information considered inconsequential."

"I suppose one cannot be too careful."

"Anything regarding Banbury's activities—certainly not."

"You knew my husband?"

He bowed. "I was the one to arrange for your excursion to Scotland."

Suddenly, the tea in my stomach soured. This man knew much. Too much. Was Sherborne certain he could be trusted?

"You were helping him?"

Oberton continued. "I tried to help him—I was too late. They struck sooner than I thought they would."

He knew the danger. Had been involved. "Why would Patrick want to participate in something so dangerous?" A question that nibbled at the back of my mind like an unwanted rat. My husband was dead and gone, I loved another. But still...Since seeing Mr. Straight, I had not been able to put my mind from it.

Tobias reached over and took my hand. "We don't have to talk about this."

"No, it's all right. I assure you."

Lord Oberton conceded. "It wasn't a dangerous job. Not at first. It was never supposed to be so. Just a little informing to the Crown. Simple work. Nothing that would put him in so deep." Lord Oberton shrugged. "But a situation took a turn. Debts were called, demanded. We didn't know at the time just how far Banbury's coils had reached until the python squeezed. That's when I rushed to relocate him."

I grimaced at the thought of the massive serpent, both intelligent and evil.

"I wasn't swift enough. He insisted on one last job and tragically was betrayed by one of our own."

I thought of Mr. Straight's final words. He'd seen the list of names and knew from there, who had betrayed him. Would my Patrick have guessed as well? He'd not had the chance. And now both men were dead.

Tobias sat back in his chair. "Will you tell us who is the turncoat?"

"It is considered heresy until I can prove it. As it is, I am the only witness. Or was." He shrugged.

He was there? Tobias tossed his napkin to the table. "*You* were a witness?"

Lord Oberton ignored his query. "Bennington. Our turncoat is Lord Bennington. Besides his estate, he owns all of the land, including the village. So..."

I recognized the name, but from where? He allowed us to piece the rest together. Tobias gave me a significant look before stating what he figured. "Bennington's estate is on the other side of the village, mere miles from Burtins. Wait, are you saying that Bennington betrayed both Patricks?"

"Exactly so." A clock chimed nine o'clock in the morning. "I imagine he is enjoying quite an engaging meeting with Colonel Humes about now. "Thanks to you, Chinworth, the Crown has the man they've been hunting for. All we needed was for you to force the bugs from the woodwork, as it were."

"I was used?" Tobias was none too happy. "In what way?"

Lord Oberton waved the butler to pour more coffee. "I see I've put you off, sir. Do calm yourself, it was not intentional. We did not know you would suddenly travel to Burtins. The situation merely became useful. We knew your presence there would set things in motion."

"No one thought to tell me?"

"I wasn't authorized until now." "And we needed to see whose side you were on. What you would do…"

"What? Authorized by whom?"

"Now that is not for you to know."

"You are telling me that Bennington used my estate as a holding place for the cache?"

He nodded. "He had your father's approval, and that fact doesn't bode well for him."

Tobias sighed. "Man's greed is dangerous."

"Ever has it been."

"Cecily and Tessa might have been caught in the cross hairs. Thank God they got out in time."

"Joseph's guards are worthy men. They performed their duty." He sipped his coffee and spoke in my direction. "Bennington deceived your husband years ago. I had no proof except for what I saw. I'm sorry that it's taken years to find him guilty. Guilty of something else, but still. He is set to lose everything. His estate—well, everything. He will go to prison."

Like Tobias's father.

"When I was shown the list of names you took from your steward, Cummins, I knew in an instant."

What had Mr. Straight said? He saw the list before he died—he knew who had deceived him. It was Bennington. His name wasn't there. The omission had informed him before he'd taken his last breath.

The list of men who had been killed or had lived through an attempt sickened me. I spoke aloud. "Of what purpose was such a list..."

"Be enemy or friend, anyone who stands in the way of the forthcoming fortune was dispensable."

"Ironic that my Uncle's name should be listed."

"Is it?" Lord Oberton had a strange look on his face.

Tobias's eyes shuttered. "Tell me he wasn't involved..."

"You think he knew?"

"He's been sending us messages for the past two years."

"Why did he not say?"

"Probably because he was sworn to secrecy on the value of his life if he revealed it to anyone, including you."

"Because..."

"Remember, we didn't know yet that you could be trusted. Your brother Samuel intercepted a message and..." the man took a bite of toast and chewed. "I'm sorry, Chinworth. When we learned that Samuel had died accidentally, we were more than a little relieved. He was a loose cannon. Tried to kill your uncle when he'd recognized his handwriting. He thought he had killed him and we allowed him to believe so. Your brother was shrewd; I'll give you that. We announced Mull's death to the London papers to keep any further threat away, hoping that the center of this operation would give us time before he realized Mulls survived."

"But Bennington..."

"Yes, the fraud Bennington. Caught wind that your uncle survived from the rat Cummins. We expected it. Your housekeeper is a gem, however. She was able to keep the truth from him for a few months."

"She kept his survival from my steward?"

"Wasn't hard to do since the man was a drunkard who was too fond of your wine cellar."

"Mrs. Fredrickson must be rewarded."

The man's eyes glinted with humor. "I agree. Understand that he was not an integral part. Just a good soul that wanted justice. He loves Burtins and its tenants. His job was a small one, but as Tessa knows, even small jobs, though important, can grow beyond our imaginings. Sometimes for the worse, as what happened with your husband."

Tobias picked up his fork and scooted a piece of meat around his plate. "I hope he did not come under any crossfire at Burtins last night."

Lord Oberton's brows rose. "He did not vacate the premises? Did you not send him a message?"

"He refused to leave." Tobias shrugged. "I couldn't force him."

Oberton stood. "Then let us hope for the best and celebrate that this particular situation is finally under control."

Admiration for the man welled within me. So many questions had been answered.

"Anytime you'd like to join us, Chinworth, we could use a man like you."

"This Chinworth has had enough of intrigues and seeks a different path."

"Very well. Do inform the staff have you any needs." He bowed. "Mrs. Audlington—er—Miss Smith. I wish you well."

"I thank you—for everything. I have learned much this day."

"I hope you can put the past to rest."

"Yes."

Lord Oberton exited the room.

Tobias and I turned to each other. There was so much said, I could scarcely take it in.

Tobias began. "I promise to continue to set things aright at Burtins, but for now, I believe we need to return to Mayfield. Since it seems we are finally safe. I've much to manage there." He stood. "I can't believe the scoundrel was Bennington. I've only met the man twice in my life. I suppose I shouldn't be surprised at my father's connections. I may not have been in his social circle, but Father and Samuel were—it is disgusting. Perhaps that is why he had no conscience. He would hurt anyone or anything in his way." Tobias sighed. "He may be the titled gent in charge of the cache's movements, but he wasn't the only guilty man. There are too many to count, according to Lord Sherborne."

"Do you think your father was trying to help?" I didn't know what to make of him.

"I can't know for certain. He's lied too many times."

"But we can hope."

"Yes, Tessa. We can always hope."

Chapter Fifteen

We spent another short day at Westhill Park. Lord Oberton played an exceptional host, his purpose being to ply my mind for any and all information. It had frustrated Tobias but I understood. Had he not said that the smallest bit of information could be useful? I answered as best as I could. As thought, I knew nothing of import.

All told, the remainder of my time at Burtins had been rather quiet and uneventful. Nothing happened outside of Cecily's healing. Gaining all he could, Lord Oberton provided a comfortable coach to take us back to Mayfield. A generous gesture.

When Cecily slept, Tobias took my hand within his—would I ever grow accustomed to his touch, his glance, his regard?

Joseph's guards remained with us until we parted ways at luncheon at a coaching inn. Butterton was another ten miles away, and the men would return to Joseph.

Soon, we were back at Mayfield and Tobias threw himself into work and I became Cecily's teacher. Her young mind was eager for engagement. We spent many quiet evenings by the fire.

Tobias continued to offer gentle embraces before we retired, but he said nothing else and made no offer of marriage. His passionate words spoken when we'd reunited had settled within his gaze and a few murmured loving words. He felt the same. I'd hoped he would have sealed his love by now but—

I turned my focus from him to the snapping fire. The chill of November had slipped in freezing draughts about the large rooms. It was hard to stay warm. I longed for his arms to wrap around me with solid reassurances concerning our future. I would have plied him on the subject if he had not been so busy and exhausted. Immediate dangers were eliminated, and his concerns had firmly settled on finding his missing nephew. But one did not take a woman's heart without a forthcoming promise. But what could I do? I didn't want to leave, felt no compulsion to do so. But we could not continue like this either.

I must have stared too long in the fire. I thought he'd left the room to retire. He slipped next to me and gently bumped my shoulder with his. "Something is wrong."

I stiffened and turned to face him. "Is there? Another threat to your life?"

"Perhaps the threat is here." He placed a hand over his heart. "I fear losing you."

"Do you?" I feared the same. So much.

His eyes warmed as his hand slid from the place over his heart and into my hand. "There are things I must attain—I—" He paused. "I don't deserve a woman like you, Tessa. Though I do not wish it, every Chinworth has a past. I want to forget mine. Desperately."

"You are forgiven it."

"Am I? The more I take note of Father's doings and even Samuel's and Zachary's, the more I see a finger pointing back at me. I've failed to be good when I should have been." He took my other hand. "I was not in jest when I told you I would endeavor to be worthy of you."

"Worth comes from God."

He nodded. "This I know. Had I realized it sooner."

"Then..." Confusion swirled.

"I must still do the work...I wish..." He pulled from my side and walked away, his words trailing behind him.

He was in turmoil over his past. What could I do? Run after him? I did so.

"Tobias" I took his hands in mine. "I will wait. For as long as it takes."

He gathered my face between his hands and kissed me as he had the first time. *Just don't make me wait too long*...I wanted the world to know of our love. Gone were the cold draughts in this house. He warmed me through and through.

He reluctantly stepped away from me, taking a deep breath. "You are a beautiful soul, Tessa." His eyes melded into mine.

A scrape sounded like metal upon metal. His gaze shifted from mine. A nerve fluttered between us. We'd endured too many dangers. So much so, that any strange sound made our ears perk like a dog's. Perhaps it was nothing. We needed to relax more. I would diffuse the tension and soften his jaw that had instantly locked at the sound. "The staff—someone must be performing a chore of some sort."

"Tessa, none of them are required to scrape about upon anything outside. The gardener does not work at night."

He was right.

"Someone or some animal is outside that window."

I looked to where he gazed. The drapes had been closed except for a slender gap. Anyone might have spied upon us.

The window darkened with a moving shadow. The wolf hounds began to bark.

"I trust my gamekeeper has set the dogs loose and frightened him away." Tobias inched toward the window.

I laughed. "Those gentle beasts? They are foreboding in size, but they wouldn't hurt a fly. On purpose, that is."

He smirked. "You're right. I need a better guard dog." He threw his hands in the air. "It couldn't possibly be another weapons cache arriving. We've nipped that in the bud."

He approached the window and pulled back the drapery. I did not think fast enough. Was but a few moments before I realized his mistake. I reached for him.

"Get away from the "

A blast sounded—the glass shattered in front of him.

He shoved me behind him as we both threw ourselves to the ground and crawled away. The dogs barked in earnest as shouts and more gunfire erupted.

"Are you hurt?" I asked him.

"No. He missed. Get to Cecily, Tessa. Run."

I did as told and scrambled away from him. My room now connected to hers. My pistol was there. And my dagger. I'd hoped the weapons to be retired from use. But no.

Someone still wanted Tobias Chinworth dead. Realization flooded me. Something Oberton had said... *"We did not know you would suddenly travel to Burtins. The situation merely became useful. We knew your presence there would set things in motion..."*

My stomach clenched as my hands shook. I ran into my room and strapped the dagger to my leg and prepared my gun for use. I made my way to Cecily's bed—a rush of relief flooded me. She was there, sound asleep.

I approached to peer at her angelic face only to find the lump beneath the blankets naught but more blankets to make it look as though she slept. She'd sneaked out of her room. Again. She had not done so since that night the fever had taken hold and we'd found her at the Burtins ruins. Had she a bad dream? Or was it an old habit returned?

She'd been doing so well that my watch over her had grown lax. I swallowed at bile that rose in my throat. Even Tobias agreed that we needed more space between us that she might learn to use her wings—in small ways. She needed to learn how to serve herself—choose a book to read, light her own candle, etc. She would be celebrating her twelfth birthday soon.

"Cecily?"

I checked behind the privacy screen. Nay, she would not be there—not when the bundle beneath the blanket meant to deceive.

I pulled the bell-pull. The servants were no doubt awakened at this point. My maid arrived with due haste.

"Mary, Cecily is gone—perhaps wandering the estate as she used to do. Stay here in case she returns."

The young woman paled. "I heard gunfire, Miss!" Her eyes flicked to my pistol.

"It wasn't mine. Do stay, I must see to my charge. Ring the housekeeper if she's returned."

"Yes, miss." The woman wrung her hands. "What should I do if a brigand enters the room?"

"I daresay we aren't overrun with them." I winced once again at the thought that most women could not defend themselves. I picked up the fire poker by the hearth. "But if one does come after you, scream like a madwoman." Screaming was a largely underestimated action. Wasn't ladylike and therefore unacceptable behavior. Yet being inappropriately loud could save one's life.

Yet another thing I needed to teach Cecily. I ran from the room and made my way to the kitchen. She was partial to two specific places and had lately been begging the reluctant cook to allow her to bake as Mrs. Fredrickson had.

Cook stood by the large oven with hands on her hips, her mop cap askew, and an apron hastily tied.

"Have you seen Cecily?"

She shook her head with an eyeroll. "I've not seen the little imp." She clanged a pot upon the stove. "The old master wouldn't expect me to boil up soup in the middle of the night, would he?"

"Cecily is not an imp; she is the lady of the house and best you remember it." The cook winced. "Who requires soup?"

"The gamekeeper, don't he? Master Chinworth says he missed supper and suffers an attack. Likely story."

The cranky cook continued about her work, clearly affronted at being woken from sleep. Did she not care that a member of the staff had been attacked? I left her to her duty. I had no time for foul moods.

I would check the folly for Cecily. But first, Tobias needed to know. I followed the sound of voices to the library where the gamekeeper did indeed recline upon a leather chair, a deep gash to his head, and otherwise rather pale and faint.

Tobias turned at my entry. "I've sent for the magistrate and the constabulary." He paused. "Where is Cecily?"

I hastily explained. "I found a bundle of bedclothes to make it look as though she slept. She has sneaked from her room."

"Dear God, not again. Not tonight!" He shouted. "John, stay with him and tend to his needs. I must find my sister."

"Did he catch the man that shot at you?"

"Indeed no. I hope he is gone for Cecily's sake."

My blood ran cold. "Check the folly."

"Right, of course."

We slipped through the portico doorway and into the cold night air. Why would she venture out of doors on such a freezing night? Would she? Should not one of us be searching the house? I clenched my jaw. One step at a time. I had to trust my instinct.

We found her, shivering, perched upon the folly steps, a note clutched in her hands. "He didn't come. Father didn't come."

Tears spilled down her cheeks. "He told me to meet him here and I did!"

I sank beside her and wrapped my arm around her shivering shoulders. Tobias took the note from her hands. His eyes steeled as he scanned the words and pocketed the note. He bent and gathered Cecily in his arms.

"My darling sister. Next time you hear from Father, let me know about it, will you? Why did you think you needed to sneak away?"

"Because everyone is saying that he is a bad man and I didn't think you would let me."

She was probably right about that.

We edged along the dark corners of the estate, keeping our words soft and cheerful for her sake.

"Did you see anyone? Talk to anyone? Hear anything?"

"Yes. A tall, fair-haired man, as fair-haired as I—was running away. He was *poaching,* Tobias. I'm sure of it."

Tobias nodded. "As the gamekeeper told."

"Do you think Father meant to come?"

"He isn't allowed to leave the gaol, Cecily. He awaits trial."

"The gaol sounds like a terrible place."

Tobias and I shared a look. "He desired to make things right, sweetheart. He's making amends."

She wrinkled her nose. "I hope he hasn't done anything very bad."

But it was. Very bad. How to tell one so young as she?

"We shall pray for him, you and I. God knows how to take care of him better than anyone else."

Then I saw the scoundrel. The man with fair hair, tall and lean, slipping behind the stables. Tobias hadn't noticed. "Tobias." I whispered. "Get inside."

"What is it?"

"Trust me, Tobias. Run for the portico. Now." He was a target and he held fast to Cecily. It wouldn't take but a moment for the man to aim and fire at both of them.

"Tessa—don't!" He shouted as he made a dash for the door."

I hadn't vowed to love and obey him—yet. Though my heart pounded from my chest, I pressed ahead. I stepped softly to the stables, easing around the opposite side just as a shot fired, its boom reverberating throughout my body. I paused when I heard a raspy voice speak.

"Not here, you wretched fool! I said Butterton Hall, not Mayfield."

"But you said Chinworth—"

"Not that Chinworth, you ignorant wretch. You got it all backward. I've never known such a lout as you."

I thought to fire my weapon and mayhap make them think they were caught. But that would be foolish. Would only draw attention to myself.

"Didn't he say he'd be here—at Mayfield? Tonight?"

"That all you remember?"

"I was to shoot him. He was to be here."

"No. You was to shoot him when he got to Butterton Hall."

Had Tobias' father planned escape? And his murder would follow? I cringed. Would that he stayed in jail instead. Had he really planned to steal Cecily away? To what kind of life?

The man grunted. "Get out of here and lay low for a while before you're caught. We need to make a new plan."

"I'm not sure I want to be part of your plan, Toffer."

"Eh?"

"Maybe I got a better offer on the table, so to speak." He ground out a bitter laugh. "Good thing I missed the gentleman."

"You're an idiot. What are you talking about?"

"Why do I do anything for anyone? Fortune. Same as you, Toffer. Good thing I didn't off either of them."

"Someone is going to off you."

"Let him try."

I pressed into the dark shed and hid behind a stack of hay, palms slick with sweat despite the cold. The pound of feet sounded nearby. Was it Tobias? Or another?

I'd not obeyed his directive to follow him into the house. I should have known he would deposit Cecily within and come after me.

"Someone's coming—get out of here, fool! Meet me at the—" his words trailed off as they ran, the information lost to the wind that chilled every part of me, body and soul. Would the threats never end?

"Tessa!" Tobias hissed. "Tessa!"

If they'd heard him, knew it was Tobias, would they still have shot at him? The man was right, they were not only evil, but they were also idiotic. As it was, Tobias needed to learn some survival skills from Joseph. He should have approached quietly, with more caution. "I am here. In the shed. They are gone."

"They?" He came closer. "There was more than one?"

"Two at least."

"Tessa." He approached until he was an inch from my nose. "Don't ever do that again. Do you promise?"

"I promise, Tobias Chinworth, that I would do anything to protect the ones I love. Anything."

"Tessa." My name came out in a puff of fog. He placed his hands on either side of my shoulders, his eyes like steel, his words as firm. "I make the same promise. But do protect my heart by not putting yourself in danger, will you?" He leaned in and pressed a light kiss to my lips.

"They meant to kill your father, Tobias. He was to be here—only there was some misunderstanding…"

"Wait, you heard a conversation?"

"I did. You weren't the target, your father was, only he was supposed to be targeted at Butterton Hall, not here." I had thought the threat that caused us to go to Burtins was not over. In this case, I was wrong.

"This makes absolutely no sense. Why Butterton Hall?"

I shivered. "I don't know. I only caught scraps of information." He grasped my hand and tugged me back to Mayfield's much warmer drawing room. "Wait here while I check on Cecily." He left me still shaking with cold by the snapping fire. I could have lost both Cecily and Tobias this night. I squeezed my eyes shut at the real possibility. Twould have been a living nightmare. I could not bear it. Not again.

Tea had been brought, and as I'd heard Lady Sherborne say many a time, tea was a mercy. I agreed. Especially tonight. I poured a cup and added cream. The house was abuzz with many new staff who were lingering about with open ears and scenarios of what had happened.

A moment later, Tobias shouted down the hall—"Check every window, every door. Lock them. Bolt everything."

I wondered if some of the staff would vacate their positions out of fear. I could not blame them.

He returned and I poured a cup of tea for him. He did not touch it.

"How is Cecily?"

"She doesn't know about the shooting. She is disappointed not to see Father tonight." He shrugged. "I don't know how to help her. She is crying. I've ordered hot cocoa for her." He threw his hands in the air. "I don't know why Father would do this to her. And how did he get a message to her?"

"Are you sure it's from him? Maybe someone wrote in his name?"

"It's definitely his handwriting."

"Ah." So his plan to come here before Butterton Hall had been correct.

"More importantly, how did he manage to get this message to Cecily under our noses? And why didn't she tell one of us?" He paced the room. "All these months I've worked so hard to gain her trust."

I stood. "She does not realize that, despite what she knows about your father, even that she should not trust him. She loves him." I thought of my own dear departed father. "He does love her, I am sure of it."

"He needn't be selfish."

No. Indeed not.

"I must ride to the jail tonight. Make sure he is still there. I pray he is, since he failed to show."

"Take someone with you?"

"I don't know who." He rubbed a hand through his hair. "The staff, including my new footman, is afraid."

"You've sent for the magistrate. He will come—and perhaps bring information regarding your father. Wait for him. Then go in the morning when it's safer to ride to the village."

"You are right. If he didn't manage to break out, he wouldn't be going anywhere. If he did, I wouldn't be able to find him."

"I'll see to Cecily. She shouldn't be alone right now." I turned to go, but Tobias reached for my arm in a gentle grasp. "About earlier, my love, we will talk more soon." He kissed my cheek.

I knew at that moment that I would wait for him as long as he needed.

Chapter Sixteen

The magistrate was furious. "No, indeed, Mr. Chinworth had not escaped!" He clapped his large, gloved hands together, as though we'd lost our senses. I'd thought the man fair, with a good reputation. Why did he behave thus? Twas confusing to say the least.

He stepped closer to Tobias. "No, indeed, I have not seen or captured two suspicious figures about Butterton or the village. No, indeed." His hands came together again as his face reddened with frustration. "What I'm not sure of is you, sir." He pointed a finger at Tobias's chest. "Mayhap like father like son, eh?" He cleared his throat while maintaining a pointed stare. "Time will tell."

"Lord Sherborne can attest to my character, sir."

"Can he? I'll not take your word for it." He grinned. "Perhaps I'll visit him when I leave here."

"By all means, do. I hope you will see that I am not my brothers and Father." Tobias held his calm. "About Father's trial. Can you tell me if there are any developments? When is it to take place?

"Nay, sir, I'll not say a word to you about it though you may grovel at my feet. Under hat, mind you. Under hat! Must keep it mum."

"What about the fact that I was shot at? Will you search that out at least?"

The large man squeezed his walking stick and gave it a generous tap on the floor. "Poacher's gun misfiring. Your imagination has run wild, Chinworth," He huffed. "As for the rest of what you ask..."

Tobias grimaced. "Yes. I know. Under hat."

"Old Liza says it's going to snow." He opened the door and cast a glance to the sky. "Nothing like snow to get one in the mood for the holidays and all that." He turned back to Tobias. "You must understand, Mr. Chinworth. I trusted your father implicitly. In light of recent events, I do not know who I can trust any longer. From Butterton to London, Banbury's scheme's have put a pox upon my life and work. I am tired. I have been called a fool by the constabulary for not knowing information sooner. I've been touted as 'ridiculous' in my club in London. Ignorant of the weevils in my meat and bread." He puffed a great breath of air. "I don't know the Chinworths as I thought, and it wounds me." He pressed a hand to his heart. "I've known you since you were a lad. I've seen you come up. But a man will do what a man designs to do and I'm left to juggle his doings with the rule of law."

Tobias was generous. He bowed. "I understand. Let me know if I can help you in any way. The Banbury case is too large for anyone to handle, no matter how small the village."

The magistrate seemed surprised by his humility. "I know I can trust Sherborne."

"As do I."

"Well then. Good day." He gave a swift nod to me and I returned a swift curtsy.

The butler closed the door behind the man.

I drew my shawl closer about my shoulders. It had grown even colder. "That was quite a speech he gave."

"Not at all." Tobias strode to the dining room with long steps while I followed. "I waited up all night for the man. He simply doesn't want to help me. I'm not surprised."

"Oh? Are you certain about that?" I thought the man merely overwhelmed.

He turned to face me, his eyes burning. "I'm a Chinworth, Tessa." He swallowed as if to let that sink in. "My family name has fast gained quite a terrible reputation." He looked me directly in the eye. "If you choose to take my name, you might never live down the gossip. You will be tied to me, and the deeds my Father committed."

I took a plate from the buffet, filled it with toast and egg, and calmly sat. Did he realize what he'd just said? "Pardon, dearest Tobias." It was my turn to look him directly in the eye. "But I have not received a proposal of marriage."

He ran a hand through his unruly hair. "I—dash it." He strode from the room, and I ate my breakfast alone, hardly tasting a bite.

I wasn't quite sure what to do. Perhaps saying nothing would have been better. I hadn't intended to sound so sarcastic. We were both overly tired from the night before. We were both irritated with the magistrate's lack of concern. And I was not about to walk away from Tobias in his greatest trial. I wanted to weather it with him. No matter what lies ahead.

I took a sip of tea, not certain I could eat food just now. I'd been as plain as he. And he'd run from the room. I dissected an egg with my fork, allowing the yolk to run across the toast.

Cecily finally went to sleep last night after a good cry. I'd stayed awake, by her side the night through. Indeed, our emotions were raw. Too raw.

We were supposed to be out of danger and focused on finding Tobias's nephew. I placed my elbow on the table and leaned my chin in my hand. I closed my eyes, trying not to let discouragement sway me. I pushed the plate across the table and leaned my head across my arms. I could sleep for days, weep for days. I loved him. Why did it have to be so hard?

A moment later, I heard Tobias reenter the room. At first, I thought it naught but the maid to clear away the food. But it wasn't. His warm hand spread across the back of my neck and rubbed.

"Are you asleep, my love?" He had calmed.

I lifted my head, a rogue tear slipping down my face. He knelt by my chair. "I have not taken care of your heart as well as I ought. Already, I fail. I've much to learn. Forgive me."

Another tear betrayed me.

He pulled something from his pocket and held it aloft. "Will you do me the honor of becoming my wife?" A ring rested in his palm, a bright sapphire wrapped in gold. Love filled his eyes.

"I'd planned to wait until Christmas. But I find I cannot wait a moment longer. I don't deserve you—you know this. But I ask all same."

He'd left the room to retrieve a ring. Not because he was angry…"Yes, Tobias. With all of my heart." I couldn't stop the flow of tears.

He took my left hand and placed the ring on my finger. "This will be my promise of marriage. I don't know when we can tie the knot," he smiled, "but you have my promise all the same. I love you." He wiped the tears away with his thumbs and pressed a kiss to my lips. "Go get some sleep. I'll have lunch sent up in a few hours. Don't worry about Cecily. I'll take care of her today."

"I can help, Tobias."

"No. You need to sleep." He pulled me up. "Someone needs to look after you for a change." He wrapped his arms around me and held me close. We stood in the soft silence and let peace pour over us. I might have fallen asleep on his chest. One day, I would.

The drama of the previous night faded as the assailants hadn't returned and the plot to murder Tobais's father hadn't come to fruition. I recounted what I overheard the men say a few more times. Tobias feared the men would do him harm, but the magistrate would not set an additional guard to Mr. Chinworth's cell. Perhaps the magistrate was correct in this matter. If there were men, and there were, they were long gone by now.

We endeavored to do what we must—and that was to wait. Tobias managed Mayfield, I taught Cecily and readied for

Christmastide, and Lord Sherborne assisted in the hunt for the missing babe. He was still not to be found.

One thing we could not understand was why? Of what great import was a wee babe to anyone but the Chinworths?

On one cold, December night after Christmas, Tobias would find out who and why. I'd been sent to have supper with Cecily in our rooms due to the sensitive nature of a certain Lord Camden's visit. Lord Camden of Butterton Hall. A tumultuous meeting occurred.

I'd never seen Tobias so dismayed, so out of temper. He was furious. We watched Lord Camden retreat on his horse from Mayfield. He'd left Tobias with a threat if he told anyone what they'd discussed. "I must find the box, or we might never find the boy—or worse. He is the one who has stolen my nephew! He bargains with life!" His voice broke. "We can tell no one, do you hear me, Tessa?" Urgency filled every fiber of his being. "We cannot tell a soul."

He endlessly paced before the fire. I could not coax him to take tea, to sit, or talk anything through. Once, he paused with a glimmer of tears in his eyes. "Lord Camden does not realize it, but something he said tonight made me realize something rather awful."

"What is it, Tobias?"

Fists pressed against his unwanted emotion. "My past is catching up with me. You may wish to end our engagement."

"I think not."

"You don't know what I've done..."

"Tell me then?"

"If I do, you will see the rogue in your eyes every time you look at me. I couldn't bear it."

"I can very well guess what kind of rogue you were." I laughed.

"It isn't humorous, Tessa."

"No. But I would have you understand the nature of forgiveness." I rose to meet him and pressed a kiss to his cheek. "It is given without cost."

"Lord Camden mentioned his niece had arrived for an extended visit. One Jane Hartford."

Understanding dawned. "And this Jane Hartford—was one of your many conquests?"

He shrugged. "Not exactly that, but I may have misled her for a reason." He paced once again. "I was sent by Father to gain her father's trust…and…"

"You got into her good graces to do so."

"I am ashamed. So ashamed."

Fear began to rise within me. I couldn't help it. "Has she reason to have a claim upon you?"

"Good gracious, no. Though if we cross paths, I can't imagine she will be pleased to see me. Her father tossed me out on my backside." He grimaced at the memory. "And earned me my father's ire."

The work of pleasing Mr. Chinworth seemed to come with a steep price. But Tobias had not stopped to consider one thing. "Those men—that shot at you. Remember? Your Father was the target. Only he was to be shot at Butterton Hall, not here. At Camden's residence. Do you think Lord Camden—"

He didn't let me finish. "I don't know what to think. The man isn't good. Anyone willing to kidnap a babe can't be. As for being a threat to my father—I don't know. I got the feeling that he was quite under Father's thumb, not the other way around."

"I wonder if he promised to help him escape from the gaol, and...would see him eliminated."

"That can't be right. He would want to keep Father alive. He knows where the box of papers is, purportedly. The man seemed desperate, no, crazed to find them."

"Crazed enough to steal away your nephew."

"What are we going to do, Tessa?"

I took his hand and he let me guide him to the settee. "We should pray."

"You are right."

He could not speak, so I did. We sat there in the quiet for a little longer. How long would it take for him to fully understand forgiveness? Guilt ate at him while evil persisted in attacking the Chinworth family. We began to pray together each day at dawn, again at eventide.

Our spirits strengthened. After days upon days of searching for the box of papers, Tobias decided to call upon Lord Sherborne. Informing him of the situation between Tobias and Lord Camden was worth the risk it posed. I prayed Lord Sherborne could do something, anything to help in this impossible circumstance. Tobias simply couldn't find the box of papers. We'd turned his office inside and out to no avail.

But just as he saddled his horse, the man himself came riding in, along with Joseph and dear Emmaline. We were overjoyed to see them; I could sense they bore ill tidings. They were sober, serious.

Lord Sherborne bowed. "I'm sorry to be the one to deliver the news, Tobias. Your father was attacked in his cell. He is deceased."

"Dear God." Tobias knees buckled as he dropped to a chair. "I warned them it could happen. I warned the magistrate."

"Yes, you did." Lord Sherborne said. "I ordered an additional guard despite his reticence. Your father might still have been involved in his dealings from the gaol. Another cache of supplies? Weapons? I do not know. Yet."

Joseph folded his arms. "The guards have been taken for questioning." He dashed a look to Sherborne and back to Tobias. "But you must know that they were knocked unconscious. We believe them innocent."

Lord Sherborne continued. "He'd begun to comply, so I thought. Maybe that's why they killed him."

Tobias swallowed at that. I hated watching him endure this news. He'd reckoned with his father's guilt some time ago. Had sought every kind of amends he knew to make. Had given his life over to God. He understood that his father had the gallows before him, in the near future. That he'd played a very dangerous game that nearly killed us both. And more. The tragic news was no surprise, but still. He loved his father.

"It is over." Tobias ran a hand through his hair. "He is gone. God have mercy on his soul."

Joseph put a hand on his shoulder. "He did try to fix his mistakes, the wrong way, perhaps. But all the same. God overflows with mercy."

I prayed that Mr. Chinworth's final moments were filled with just that. Mercy.

Tobias stood. "What do I do know?"

Lord Sherborne nodded to Joseph. "The magistrate desires you collect his body forthwith. He does not desire to keep it or investigate."

"Of course not."

"The good vicar has offered to keep vigil on your behalf. He is willing to perform the burial ceremony as soon as you require it." Sherborne took a packet from his interior pocket. "He had this with him. I thought you'd want to have it."

Tobias untied the wrapping. He held a miniature painting in his hand, encased in gilded wood. "Mother."

I peered over his arm. "She was much like Cecily."

Tobias closed his eyes. "Cecily. I have to tell her the news."

Joseph nodded. "Tis why I brought along Emmaline. She and Tessa can help."

"Thank you, Cousin."

"I am very sorry, Tobias."

Sad tidings surrounded by evil, mystery, doubt, and, of all things, love.

Chapter Seventeen

I was grateful to see dear Emmaline again. Cecily was a changed girl and I thought twas good for Emmaline to see the healing that had taken place. Cecily had wept at the news of her father's death. A few hours later, she admitted to praying that the angels would take him to heaven where he wouldn't have to be sorry any longer.

Miraculously, the young girl was at peace, though she clung to her brother's neck tightly as he hugged her before she fell asleep.

That night, Emmaline returned with Joseph to the Sherborne's estate and Tobias and I wandered the halls as though on a walk. Since the night Tobias was shot upon, I'd not stopped wearing my dagger. I was hard-pressed to leave my pistol hidden in my room.

And I could not stop thinking about the many threats upon his life. His name had been on Cummin's and Lord Bennington's list—merely because he was a Chinworth and in the way. When that came to an end, we thought all threats were gone. We hadn't been surprised to find Mr. Chinworth a target after his dealings—and yet—I could not let go of the thought that Tobias's life might still be in danger. My skin crawled betimes. Was he being watched? Was he within the sites of an aim? I couldn't shake the feeling. Was well that I did not.

"Tobias—what did you do with the message—the one that required us to leave for Burtins?"

"I tossed it, why?"

"Do you think it still might be of import?" Had this not been the reason for our initial escape? I felt as though it had been forgotten under the weight of everything else that had happened. I could not conceive losing him. Not now. Not ever.

"Sherborne and I believe the note was a trick of Father's to get me away to Burtins. It worked. I'll never know the depths of his manipulations." A sob filled his throat. "I loved him despite all."

I squeezed his hand.

If what he and Sherborne suggested were true, twas a cruel trick to play upon a son. What had the note said? *"The Chinworth name will fall in the rubble of its stone. Not one will remain. Pay or die."*

Pay or die? Pay or die. "Tobias? Have you made payments to anyone? Apart from Lord Camden blackmailing you for your nephew, has he required payment perhaps?"

"No. I tried to offer him money in exchange for the babe—but he couldn't be bribed. Said the fortune coming to him was far greater than I offered."

I repeated the words aloud of the threat made.

"Tessa, I see that you are still concerned. I believe all threats are gone—done for. My gamekeeper hasn't noted anything since the night he was attacked."

"Is this the same gamekeeper who was present for the cache smuggling?" He was but one man.

"He is not. I hired him just when Father left...but the man came well recommended." He put an arm around my shoulder. "Please don't worry any longer. I beg you. Sherborne sends a few men to come walk the property a few times each week. Again, nothing. No more activity is occurring. We can be at ease."

I wished I could trust his answer—and Lord Sherborne's. I hadn't known we were being "looked after" again—for at least a few days of the week.

"You are certain, Tobias?" I looked into his eyes, filled with both peace and grief all at once. "I don't want to lose you too."

He paused our steps and turned me to face him. He lifted his hand and cupped my cheek. "I wish I could promise you every tomorrow that will ever exist, but I can only give you the tomorrows that are promised to me by God himself. He numbers my days, my love. And yours. Even if the worst shall happen, know that my heart has only truly been yours, whether I die tomorrow or when I'm one hundred and three." He smirked. "You probably won't want me when I'm that old."

I laughed. "You are impossible."

"Impossibly in love with you, Tessa."

A maid walked by with an ash bucket. Off to clean out my fireplace to rekindle a new one.

"Unfortunately, the village is beginning to gossip about our relationship."

Gossip could be evil.

"Shall we marry soon and do away with their wicked minds?"

He smiled. "I believe we shall." We made our way to the cozy library downstairs. "The bans have been read—weeks ago. The vicar is ready as soon as we are."

"I'd marry you this night if it were possible."

"Tessa..." The warmth in his eyes heightened. "We'll bury my father first—and then—"

I wrapped my arms fully around his waist as he held me. Burying a parent was a most difficult, emotional task.

"We won't be able to go on a honeymoon tour..."

"I don't need a honeymoon. I just want to be with you."

"Pardon me, sir." The butler bowed. "Miss Smith." He held a silver tray bearing a message. "The boy Matthew Dawes just delivered this. From Goodwyn Abbey."

Tobias plucked the note from the tray. "Thank you. Have tea sent, will you?"

"Yes, sir."

He opened the missive. "Oh my." His face paled. "Do you remember my telling you about one Jane Hartford of Chillham?"

"Lord Camden's niece or some such?"

"The very same. Sherborne has informed me that attempts have been made on her life—and she is very much in danger. She must flee Butterton Hall. The solicitor aims to help her—as does Dr. Rillian."

"The danger hasn't left Butterton—but shifted to Butterton Hall…" I looked at Tobias for answers. "But why?"

"Lord Camden is a schemer like my father. I must go to Goodwyn Abbey. It seems I owe them some information."

"What do you know, Tobias?"

"These last several weeks, as I've taken note of every transaction, every letter saved, I found some messages I did not expect. I thought them moot since the girl's father is dead and gone."

"Jane's father?"

"Yes."

"But what does he have to do with Banbury?"

Tobias looked me straight in the eye. "That's the thing. Her father wouldn't have anything to do with him. The vicar wouldn't be manipulated or tempted by fortune."

"Then why is Jane in danger?" I did not think women to be involved, but that was foolish thinking.

"She shouldn't be. Not at all." He reached into his pocket that was forever bulging with important papers he dared not lose from sight. "I found these letters—that might explain it. Some, at any rate. Perhaps she can fill in the blanks. All I know is, this woman has no reason to be in danger."

He began to pace. "Unless she heard something. Or was in the wrong place at the wrong time—or worse. Accepted the bribe that her father would not."

"Lord Sherborne knows of this?"

"He does. He asks me to come by sunrise." He grasped my hands. "I must apologize to the woman, Tessa. She will hate me on sight, I expect. I am prepared for it."

"Shall I go with you?"

"My dearest love, I will go alone, and I will be safe. You will stay with Cecily? Her heart will be sore when she remembers Father's death." He grimaced. "I hate leaving her at a time like this, but Miss Hartford's life is at stake. I will do what little I can."

"Of course." I hugged him again.

We drank a cup of tea, prayed, and made our way to our rooms. I couldn't sleep a wink, nor shrug the fear that the danger to Jane was the same for Tobias.

When I saw him next, it was as though a great burden had rolled from his shoulders. He rode back that evening, and came straight to my side. Peace flooded his expression. "It is good to right wrongs. The right way." His smile was gentle. "Miss Hartford forgave me—and my information explained much."

"It helped then. Good."

"Jane Hartford is to marry the solicitor who came to her aid. A Mr. Stevens. They wed in the morning—and after, we will bury my father."

"New beginnings and endings—all at once."

"Yes. But I was hoping that while the vicar is dressed for one wedding, that he might officiate two?" He bit his bottom lip as he posed the question. "What do you say?"

"We have already been long delayed, I feel."

"You consent?"

"Absolutely. I cannot wait another moment to be your wife."

He leaned his head against mine. "I've been rather sudden."

"No more than our entire story has been." I laughed.

Chapter Eighteen

Tobias and I are wed! It is a strange happening to witness the marriage of another couple, bury a man and return once again to the altar. As the vicar gracefully put it, "Life to life, love to love. Put away the old things, put on the new…"

I knew Tobias would grieve for a long time to come over the losses within the family—but I would be with him. He hadn't lost everything. We had each other—and Cecily. And one day, we hoped with all fervency, his wee nephew.

The Sherborne's set up a wedding feast—a surprise we'd not expected. How I loved having Joseph and Emmaline by my side as I'd spoken my vows to Tobias. Joseph was like a brotherly anchor to Tobias now, instead of the opposing, poor cousin.

I was glad of it. Tobias needed a brother—a good brother to stand by his side throughout the life that was to be ours, and as Tobias put it, for the time God gives us.

Lord Sherborne and Elaina were gracious hosts, sparing no good thing upon the table. And I was the recipient of a rather stunning paper bouquet given to me by Callum. Indeed, the entire table had been flooded with paper roses.

Elaina whispered in my ear, "Callum worked the night through to decorate for you. He delights in pleasing young brides."

Cecily had joined us for the feast—her smiles showed as much peace as had come upon her brother. She was truly set free from the effects of the dangerous elixir—and set free from manipulations. She embraced me with such ferocity. "Now, you will never leave me! I will have you forever!" Her glee was contagious. Our marriage was a good distraction from her father's death. If only for a short time.

Tears would come, but we would cry together, dry our tears together, and laugh again.

When we arrived back to Mayfield, we had quite another surprise in store.

The butler announced to Tobias, "A Mrs. Fredrickson and a Mr. Mulls to see you, sir."

Tobias grinned.

"Why are they here? What aren't you telling me?"

"My love. Cecily wants to bake in the kitchen and the children of Butterton could benefit from one very generous kite maker. For a year at least."

"A year?" What was he thinking? Did not Burtins require them?

"I've begun restorations on Burtins, employing ten young men of the area. When they return—when we all return—the estate will be freshened up a bit."

"You've given employment to some of the young men?"

He winked. "Most of whom are already married with little mouths to feed. Yes. I have." He led me down the hall towards the drawing room. "And I've hired a shepherd to train a few of the lads. And," he smiled again, "Mr. Ode will have the large crops and proper equipment. Once again, we aim to make Burtins self-sustaining."

I was so proud of his efforts. I loved this man. So very much. He opened the door where the old pair awaited.

Was like a holiday had descended upon Mayfield Manor. What was once a conniving place had become different. No longer did the air feel the weight of distress—but became filled with the air of hope. We would be happy. We would choose to be so, despite the length of our lives or our circumstances.

Tobias and Lord Sherborne must have been right. For no further threat came upon Tobias, though sometimes an irrational fear came upon me. I prayed, set it aside, and continued in our newfound hope.

Two weeks later, the fear surged.

Tobias shouted. He ran through the house, shouting my name. I grabbed my pistol, that I'd kept dangerously loaded and ready and met him, ready to meet the enemy with him. He panted down the hall, jacketless, breathless, hands upon his knees, a note clutched in his hands. Tears streamed down his face.

"They found him. They found my nephew." He sank to his knees. "It's horrible the way he was found, indeed. But no harm has come to him. He is safe—Jane is safe."

"Jane?" I asked. "Is she not on her honeymoon?"

"She was kidnapped on the way. Lord Camden took her to the babe. Matthew was with her. They escaped together!"

I knelt with him on the floor. "They found him."

"Praise be to God who directs our steps."

I continued his truth. "Though the enemy means it for evil, God intends good."

"Yes..." he wept, "Yes!"

EPILOGUE

Lord Sherborne gave Tobias a scrap of paper. "Look at this—see if you recognize the handwriting." The babe had two fists of Tobias's hair.

"Save me, Tessa!" He laughed.

"Easily done!" No self-defense or pistols needed. I unfolded the babe's fists and took him in my arms. The wee one laughed and clapped his hands.

After the events surrounding Jane Hartford's rescue and Butterton Hall housekeeper's admission, we'd been stunned by the turn of events. Was there still more to know?

"This handwriting looks identical to the threat I received before leaving for Burtins."

"You may be surprised to learn that this is Mr. Roth's handwriting. The housekeeper's son, Butterton's gamekeeper. As told, he murdered your father."

Tobias blinked. "He meant to kill us all."

"Retribution," I said. "For what happened to his sister." Samuel's secret wife. The one Samuel planned to murder had she not died of illness, in order to marry Emmaline for her fortune. A dastardly business.

"He very nearly managed the task last summer." Tobias handed the paper back to Lord Sherborne. "If it wasn't for Tessa, I don't know that I'd be standing here today."

Lord Sherborne bowed to me with a smile. "Mrs. Chinworth. I hear great things about your skills. I've a mind to beg your assistance."

Tobias stepped in front of me before I could answer. "Keeping her out of danger these days, old boy."

Sherborne laughed. "You mistake my meaning. I'd be honored if she would train my wife. I, too, would see her come to no harm." He pulled on his gloves to depart. "We both know that we can't always be a shield, as much as we'd like to be."

I curtsied. "I thank you, Lord Sherborne. It would be my pleasure to assist your wife in any way that I can."

"Good day." He turned to leave but I was not satisfied. Not every question had been answered.

I had to know. "What of the man that assaulted my husband? The one I helped save him from?"

"Ah—that. Yes. Lord Bennington has confessed to many things. We now suspect he was the one behind the attack."

Like Jane, my husband had been unwittingly caught in webs of other's making.

"We must be content with the unknown, as God does know everything."

The babe laughed again, a sound filled with glee. His cheeks were plump and healthy. Jane said he'd been with a wet nurse. He'd been cared for. He'd been kidnapped, but what if, in that space of time, the child was being kept safe from worse?

Lord Sherborne took his leave and Tobias lifted the boy from my arms. "He hasn't a name yet."

Mr. Mulls stepped into the room. "Why, Tobias, my nephew. This boy..." He held a finger and the babe grasped it tight. "Has the perfect grip for kite flying. Do not you think?"

"I believe I know this child's namesake."

I looked at old Mr. Mulls, his bright eyes and generous spirit. I nodded.

"What is your Christian name, Uncle?"

"Pardon?"

"The babe would like to know."

A hand over his heart, he stated, "Hezikiah Barret Mulls."

"Barrett..." We both said at once and laughed.

"What do you find so humorous?"

"Might he borrow your name, dear Uncle?"

"Oh my."

"We shall take him to the vicar directly and have him recorded as Barrett Patrick Chinworth."

Patrick...

"For the honor and bravery of three worthy gentlemen." Tobias kissed the boy's cheek.

I stood with mouth agape.

"Is that alright, my love?"

Tears threatened. "It is a gift. I thank you."

Cecily ran into the room. "How many more months, Uncle, until he can fly a kite?" She grabbed his hand and they left the room together.

Mrs. Fredrickson fetched the babe for feeding and left Tobias with his arms around me. It is well for a good man to be brave and honorable, how much more the prodigal that climbs from the pits of evil to come to the same? I tightened my hold. I would never let go.

Butterton Brides Series:

A Convenient Sacrifice
A Favorable Match
An Opportune Proposal
A Noble Gift
A Concealed Affection
An Honorable Pursuit, coming Fall of 2025

Hearts Unlocked:

Of Needles and Haystacks
Of Horse and Rider
Of Time and Circumstance
Of Hearts and Home
Of Pens and Ploughshares

Regency Hobbit Retelling:

An Unexpected Journey

Ann Elizabeth Fryer is a recent resident at Chief-End Farm in small town, Illinois where she spends her days enraptured by nature, writing stories, and corralling the puppy dogs. Ann, her husband, and their three nearly independent children are loving the farm life after many years of living in town. You can find out more about her upcoming book releases at www.annfryerwrites.com

Printed in Dunstable, United Kingdom